"You can [...] in a way [...]

Kent's voice [...] to a low, intense pitch. "There's so much I want to see done in this country, but I have to get elected first—and that means votes."

"Do you really think I could help?" Catherine asked uneasily. "I don't know...."

"Tonight, your singing, the way you got along with the guests, was fabulous. People admire you because you're Cat Devlin." He placed his hands on her shoulders and peered into her face. "And I *want* you by my side."

She looked up at him, feeling quite torn. She *could* do a lot for his campaign. She could also ruin it. The secrets about her brother's death, about the Devlin image, could do irreparable damage. She should tell him before it was too late....

And risk having him walk out of her life? She couldn't face that—not now.

SANDRA K. RHOADES began reading romance novels for relaxation when she was studying for her engineering degree and became completely hooked. She was amazed at how much fun the books are, and before long her sights were set on a career in romance writing. Colorado-born, she now lives in British Columbia with her husband and their two children. There she raises livestock, and every summer keeps a large garden.

Books by Sandra K. Rhoades

HARLEQUIN PRESENTS
917—A RISKY BUSINESS
956—BITTER LEGACY

Don't miss any of our special offers. Write to us at the following address for information on our newest releases.

Harlequin Reader Service
901 Fuhrmann Blvd., P.O. Box 1397, Buffalo, NY 14240
Canadian address: P.O. Box 603,
Fort Erie, Ont. L2A 5X3

SANDRA K. RHOADES

shadows in the limelight

Harlequin Books

TORONTO • NEW YORK • LONDON
AMSTERDAM • PARIS • SYDNEY • HAMBURG
STOCKHOLM • ATHENS • TOKYO • MILAN

Harlequin Presents first edition October 1987
ISBN 0-373-11021-9

Original hardcover edition published in 1987
by Mills & Boon Limited

CHAPTER ONE

THE familiar strains of an old Beatles' tune came from the Muzak system and unconsciously Catherine sang along. She was arranging russet chrysanthemums and baby's breath, and as a finishing touch for Hallowe'en, she added a black plastic witch on a broomstick and an orange and black striped ribbon. As she stepped back to admire her handiwork, her voice rose as the song neared its end. She didn't hear the door open as someone entered the store. The silence that followed the final stanza was a broken by an awed voice saying: 'Lord, Cat, I'll never understand how you could have given it all up!'

Startled, Catherine turned to see her friend Nancy, staring at her with an idolising expression. Grimacing slightly, she said, 'You scared me, I didn't hear you come it. Is it six o'clock already?' It was Friday and she was going out with Nancy after work for supper and a movie.

'Almost,' Nancy answered. 'I cheated and closed the gift shop a bit early. I'd have quit even sooner if I had known you were giving a concert. Come on, sing another song for me!' She came around the counter and perched on the stool Catherine kept there, her smile coaxing.

Catherine shook her head. 'Don't be silly, what if a customer comes in? They'll think I've flipped!' She removed the Hallowe'en arrangement to the refrigerator.

'Are you kidding? Hearing Cat Devlin, *live*—it

5

would make their day! You should never have quit.'
Nancy studied her curiously, shaking her head
slightly. Even with the conservative hairstyle and light
make-up her friend wore now, it was still easy to
picture Catherine in the role of a star. She had an
indefinable something about her. It wasn't simply
beauty, though she certainly was beautiful—with
glorious auburn hair surrounding a classic oval face set
with large, long-lashed, sherry-brown eyes. There was
more to Catherine than simple good looks: an aura, a
charisma, that attracted attention in a way mere
beauty never could.

Impulsively, Nancy blurted out, 'You could have
been a superstar by now.'

Catherine shrugged noncommittally, clearing away
the remnants of leaves and blossoms so she wouldn't
have to look at her friend. Nancy's curiosity about Cat
Devlin was irritating and Catherine wished she had
never given in to the impulse to confide in her. Ever
since she had found out about her career as an
entertainer, Nancy had plagued her with questions
about her previous life. Though she knew Nancy was
hurt by her refusal to discuss it, Catherine had no
intention of doing so. It was the past, dead and buried
as far as she was concerned, and she wasn't going to
dig it up simply to satisfy her friend's curiosity.

Nonetheless she felt slightly guilty about her
reticence and finally gave in to Nancy's coaxing to
sing for her. When the Muzak tape clicked into
another song, she started to sing. After a few bars,
Catherine turned away slightly, so the other girl
couldn't see her face. She had sung the ballad a
hundred times before, it had been a standard in their
act. In her mind, she could hear her brother Casey's
baritone accompanying her, and her eyes suddenly

misted over. He had been dead over five years now, and Catherine wondered if she would ever stop missing him.

As the last note died away, Catherine blinked the moisture from her eyes and turned to look at Nancy. It wasn't her friend's face that held her attention, though, but that of the man standing behind her. For a long moment, she could only stare into his keen blue eyes, still caught up in the spell of the past. Then he lifted one dark brow quizzically, the handsome planes of his face expressing his amusement.

Catherine's face flamed. Maybe in old musicals people burst into song regardless of their environment, but she felt terribly embarrassed at having a stranger find her belting one out in a flower shop. Her colour deepening, she mumbled an apology. 'I'm sorry, I didn't hear you come in.'

He ignored her embarrassment, and continued to study her, an appreciative expression in his eyes. As his gaze made a leisurely journey over her body, taking in the feminine curves only partially concealed by the denim coverall she wore, Catherine felt her face growing even hotter. 'Is there something I can help you with? I was just about to close.'

'You're very good,' he said enigmatically, and Catherine frowned. She didn't think he was talking about her voice.

'Well, she should be.' Nancy jumped into the conversation enthusiastically, flashing him a brilliant smile. 'Don't you recognise her?'

He turned back to Catherine, giving her a faint smile. 'I'm sorry, I'm afraid I don't.'

Catherine shot Nancy a quelling glance, which her friend promptly ignored.

'Surely you've heard of Cat Devlin?' asked Nancy

disregarding the furious expression in Catherine's eyes.

'Sorry, it doesn't ring a bell.'

'I'm sure this gentleman is in a hurry, Nancy,' Catherine interposed swiftly when it looked as though Nancy would continue. 'You wanted flowers?' She stepped away from the counter towards one of the display cases.

Unfortunately, he didn't take the hint and follow, but remained where he was, eyeing her curiously. 'You're Cat Devlin?'

'I was,' Catherine said curtly, then, remembering he was a customer, felt obliged to add, 'It was my stage name, I used to sing professionally. The flowers . . .?'

'Locally?'

'I beg your pardon?'

'Did you sing locally?'

'Cat and her brother were headliners in Las Vegas,' Nancy pushed her way back into the conversation. 'They were very successful. I can't imagine how you never heard of them. They were a tradition—like Wayne Newton. Haven't you ever heard *Stardust Magic*? That was their big hit. It was in the charts for ages.'

Someday I'll murder that girl! Catherine thought, glaring at her. She *knows* I don't like discussing my singing career. When it appeared that Nancy was going to continue regaling her customer with details of the Devlins, Catherine interrupted rudely by saying, 'As I said, I was about to close. If you'd tell me what you'd like . . .?'

'So, you and your brother sang *Stardust Magic*?' he asked curiously instead of answering her request.

'That's right,' Catherine said tersely. 'We were a one-hit wonder. Now, if you don't mind . . .'

He studied her a moment, his expression considering, then his gaze swept the room, alighting on an arrangement of carnations. 'That will do.' He gestured to the small bowl of flowers.

Catherine could feel his eyes following her as she walked over to the display cabinet to remove the flowers. When she turned back he was still watching her, a pensive light in his eyes. 'How long has it been since you sang professionally?' he questioned as she brought the flowers over to the counter.

'Did you want a card?' Catherine asked curtly, ignoring his question. Her brown eyes met his in a cold stare.

For several seconds he held her gaze, the temperature in his own eyes dropping radically. 'I think not, just the flowers.' The coldness in his voice matched her own. Taking his wallet from the inner pocket of his suit jacket, he withdrew a rectangular plastic charge card and laid it on the counter. As Catherine slipped some tissue paper round the arrangement, she surreptitiously eyed the card. Kent Latimer—she covertly read the name and recognised it immediately. No wonder he had looked vaguely familiar! He had his law offices on the upper floors of this building and probably passed by the store almost every day. Besides, his picture appeared frequently in the paper as he was one of Vancouver's aldermen.

His name told her one more thing about him, and Catherine felt her heart sink. Though he had never entered the shop before today he was one of her best customers. His secretary had placed hundreds of phone orders in his name during the three years that Catherine had been in business—and now that he had finally come in person, she had been horribly rude to him.

Feeling chagrined, she set the arrangement on the counter in front of him, bestowing a warm smile on him as she did so by way of a peace offering. Unfortunately, she wasn't allowed to discover whether the smile would have been returned because as she moved her hands away from the flowers, she accidentally knocked the container of water that had earlier held chrysanthemums and sent the icy liquid cascading straight down the front of Kent Latimer's previously immaculate trousers.

'Oh, no!' she exclaimed, staring in paralysed horror at the water dripping from his slacks on to what were obviously hand-made shoes. He had already taken out his handkerchief and was rubbing at the dark stain on the light grey slacks before Catherine gathered enough of her wits to say more.

'Oh, Mr Latimer, I'm terribly sorry,' she apologised starting around the counter to go to his assistance.

He held up his hand, forestalling her. 'Please, don't bother,' he enjoined in a frigid voice. Giving his trousers a final scrub with the handkerchief, he straightened. He stared at her for a moment, his attractive face set in harsh lines, then carefully picked up his credit card and slipped it into his pocket. 'I've changed my mind about the flowers. Please forgive me for having prevented you from closing on time.'

When he turned to stalk away, Catherine hastily grabbed up the arrangement and rushed after him. 'Please, Mr Latimer, take the flowers ... they're on the house. I mean, it's the least I can do ... and you must send me the bill for having your trousers cleaned. I really am very sorry.'

He turned to look at her, his expression impassive, but she knew he was still furious with her. However, he held out his hand for the bowl of carnations.

'Thank you, I will take the flowers,' he said in a clipped voice. 'Unfortunately, it's late and I really don't have time to pick any up elsewhere.' Catherine's relief that he was accepting her olive branch died a swift death as he added, 'Especially as I'll obviously have to change now.' Swinging around, he stalked out of the shop with the door banging shut behind him.

Mortified, Catherine stood there staring after him, until Nancy said from behind her, 'Catherine, how could you? I know you don't like talking about when you were a singer, but did you have to dump water all over that poor man?'

The reproach she had been flogging herself with suddenly had an outlet. As she swung around to face the other girl Catherine's eyes were blazing. 'It was an accident! And as for the other, since you know I hate talking about having been a singer, why did you tell him? I'm thoroughly sick of you. Ever since you found out I used to be Cat Devlin, you moon around me like some damned groupie! And now you've decided to shoot your mouth off to every Tom, Dick, and Harry you meet that you know the great Cat Devlin. Well, get this through your head: *Cat Devlin doesn't exist any more*. She's dead, right along with Casey Devlin. So quit trying to dig her up!'

'I thought we were friends,' Nancy remonstrated. Her bosom heaving, Catherine simply glared at her, unmoved by the tears streaking the other girl's cheeks. After a tense silence, Nancy said, 'I suppose it was a bit much to expect a big star to want to be friends with an ordinary person like me. I imagine you're ashamed for people to know what kind of company you're keeping these days.'

The unmistakable hurt in the younger girl's voice swept Catherine's anger away on a tide of contrition.

'I'm sorry, Nancy,' she said wearily. 'We *are* friends, and I had no right to say those things to you.'

'But you meant them, didn't you?'

Catherine hesitated. 'Well . . . not the way it came out. You're my best friend, but I wish you wouldn't keep harping on the fact that I used to be Cat Devlin. That part of my life is over, I don't want to even think about it any more.' The other girl was unmollified. Catherine took a step towards her, but Nancy retreated. 'Oh, for crying out loud, Nancy! I don't want to argue with you, it's just . . . couldn't you forget what I used to be? Who I used to be? Can't I be your friend Catherine Delaney, who runs a florist's?'

There was a stubborn expression on the other girl's face, but also a faint gleam in her eye. 'OK, but only if you tell me why you won't talk about it. If we're friends, then we shouldn't have secrets from one another. If you explain to me why, I'll never say another thing about you being Cat Devlin.'

Catherine looked at her, then shook her head slightly. Nancy was five years younger than she was and naturally it had influenced their relationship. Never before, though, had Catherine been so acutely aware of the gap, not just in years but in the experience that yawned between them. 'Nancy,' she said gently, 'there are some things that even best friends can't talk to each other about.'

'You're not going to tell me?'

'No, I'm not.'

'Then I don't think we're friends.'

Catherine lowered her head a moment, rubbing the nape of her neck ruefully. Her next words didn't come easily. 'If that's the way you feel about it, then I guess we aren't.'

'Fine,' snapped Nancy, and stepped briskly around

Catherine and out of the shop.

For several minutes, she remained motionless. Nancy wasn't going to be back. She knew the girl well enough to know that unless she gave in to Nancy and explained all about Cat Devlin, Nancy wouldn't forgive her. And even to preserve their friendship, she wouldn't do that.

Finally, Catherine crossed to the door and after locking it, turned the sign to Closed. 'I'm batting a thousand today,' she said to the umbrella tree positioned by the entrance. 'I just managed to lose a friend and my best customer in less than half an hour,' and promptly burst into tears.

Kent Latimer grimaced at the bulging scrapbook his secretary had just deposited on his desk, wondering how he was going to avoid looking at it without hurting the woman's feelings. He was now regretting his impulsive decision last Friday to treat Miss Hamilton to dinner, but at the time it had seemed a good idea. That day had been the middle-aged spinster's birthday and she had appeared to have no one else with whom to celebrate the occasion.

At first, conversation had been awkward. They had little in common outside their relationship as employer-employee, and business did not seem to be an appropriate topic for a celebratory dinner. Almost in desperation, Kent had related the incident at the florist's where he had obtained her birthday flowers. He had certainly hit on a topic dear to Miss Hamilton's heart, he thought wryly.

Miss Hamilton had been enthralled by the fact that her idol, Cat Devlin, was the woman from whom she had ordered so many flowers over the years—and disbelieving that her boss had never heard of the star.

Over the next hour, she had proceeded to remedy that. She had, it appeared, read everything ever written about the Devlins and, Kent thought drily, eyeing the scrapbook, saved it all.

Nevertheless, Kent admitted it had been an entertaining evening. Until then, he had suspected that the other girl in the shop had been exaggerating her friend's former popularity as an entertainer. She had understated the case, he thought, skimming through a newspaper clipping that had fallen from the scrapbook. The Devlins had had both fame and fortune during their career and from all accounts had been two of the best-loved stars ever to perform on the Las Vegas stage.

The intercom on his desk signalled just as he had decided he would waste a little time perusing Miss Hamilton's memorabilia on the Devlins. 'Yes?' he asked, having pushed down the call button.

'Your father is on line three. Shall I put him through, Mr Latimer?'

Kent made a face, then said, 'Go ahead ... good morning, Dad.'

'Kent, glad I caught you in,' said James Latimer, then without further preamble, got to the point of the call. 'I had lunch with Charlie Ames yesterday. He says it looks like McKeirnan is definitely going to step down. He thinks the Prime Minister will call the by-election to fill the seat this spring. It looks like this could be your chance. I——'

'I know about the seat, Dad,' Kent interrupted, trying to keep the edge from his voice. 'Peter and I are on top of it. We're going to go for it, but everything is still in the planning stages.'

'Well, what plans have you made so far?' his father demanded. 'Have you met Penrod yet? You're going to have to have him on your side to swing this.'

Kent's lips pressed together. 'We're kicking around several ideas. The main thing we need right now is to get me more exposure.'

'Exposure!?!' James Latimer exclaimed. 'Nonsense! What you need is the backing of the right people, like Penrod. Do you want me to invite him over to the house? Maybe make a weekend of it?'

'No, Dad, I don't,' Kent said evenly. 'To be honest with you, I don't think I want Penrod's support. He and I are at opposite ends of the political spectrum and I know that to have his backing, I would have to go along with him on some things I just couldn't agree with.' Before his father could respond, Kent continued quickly, 'Don't worry about it. I'm not without a few back-room boys of my own. Right now, what we are going to concetrate on is getting some publicity.'

'Publicity!' his father scorned, then launched into a long discourse on the political clout possessed by Mr Earl Penrod, which his son listened to with only half an ear. While he knew his father was only trying to help, Kent was annoyed nonetheless that James Latimer refused to accept that his son was perfectly capable of making his own decisions regarding his political career—and his life, for that matter.

'As for your wanting publicity,' James Latimer scoffed, 'without the right people behind you, all the publicity in the world won't get you elected dogcatcher. I may not have ever run for office, but I know what I'm talking about. You'll get elected by sitting with the boys in the smoke-filled rooms, not by having your picture spread all over the media.'

Ironically, at that moment Kent was staring at a publicity picture from a magazine, not of a politician, but of the singer, Cat Devlin. What a beautiful child she had been! Not that the woman she had become was not a beauty, but she no longer possessed that look of uninhibited joy that made the teenager so eye-catching. Was it only age that had robbed her of that *joie de vivre*?

'Well, so you agree with me? You'll meet with Penrod?' his father demanded, and Kent realised that he had nearly forgotten the man on the phone.

'No,' he said bluntly, still holding the picture. 'I have to trust my own instincts. I'm sorry, Dad, but that's the way it is. Now, I'd better be going. Say hello to Mom for me. Goodbye.' He hung up before his father had a chance to detain him with further arguments.

For several minutes, Kent continued to study the photograph. His father discounted the value of publicity in a political campaign, but Kent knew better. You could not put your ideas across if you couldn't gain the voters' attention. And it wasn't the back-room boys who could get you that attention. Perhaps here was a way of showing his father that it took something more—or someone.

Catherine tossed the pen on to her desk, stretching her arms above her head to ease her cramped muscles. She loved running the flower shop, dealing with the customers and suppliers, and working on the arrangements. The only drawback was doing the accounts. Apart from the fact that she was appallingly bad at maths, she was never comfortable demanding payment on overdue accounts. She catered to a wealthy clientele and though one would have thought that this wouldn't be a problem, if anything it seemed to make it worse. She was beginning to think that the reason her clients had so much money was because they never paid for the things they ordered! Most seemed to think nothing of allowing their accounts to fall months into arrears.

Massaging her temple, she wished she hadn't lost Kent Latimer as a customer. Not only had he ordered a lot of flowers, he had actually paid for them! Roses, forget-me-nots, orchids—they had gushed out of the shop as gifts for his girl-friends. What an idiot she had been to offend him! The worst part was she probably had even less chance of making up with him than she did with Nancy, after a week during which she had been thoroughly snubbed by the girl.

Fortunately, before she could brood on the loss of her friend for long, her assistant, Paula, came into the office. 'There's someone to see you.'

'Coming.' Catherine glanced down at her accounts and shoved her chair back, pleased at the interruption. Maybe she should hire an accountant—let someone else untangle all those numbers and send out chastising letters to the clients who wouldn't pay. The idea brought a smile to her lips as she left the office.

It died a swift death as she recognised her visitor. What was Kent Latimer doing here? Though he had never sent her the cleaning bill for his trousers, Catherine hadn't been surprised that his secretary had stopped placing orders with her.

'You wanted to speak to me?' she asked, taking her courage in both hands when she reached him, tilting her head slightly to look up at him. Close up, he was devastatingly good-looking: his features were well formed and aristocratic, the clear blue of his eyes startling against his tan. There was a certain rugged masculinity about his face that the newspaper photographs she had seen of him hadn't captured. And while she had realised he was handsome, for

some reason she hadn't expected him to be quite so
sexually attractive. But he was, extremely so. Her
smile grew strained.

'Miss Delaney, I dropped in to ask you to have
dinner with me this evening.' He smiled down at her,
exposing even white teeth that could have featured in
a toothpaste ad.

As his smile widened into a grin, she realised she
was gaping at him. Hastily she closed her mouth, but
couldn't hide the confusion in her features. 'Why?'
She said the first thing that came into her mind.

He laughed softly, a warm, male sound that affected
Catherine's pulse. 'Surely you don't need to be told
how attractive you are? I hadn't expected you to fish
for compliments,' he teased her gently, his eyes openly
admiring.

Catherine flushed deeply at his familiarity and
realised that, of course, a man with as many admirers
as Kent Latimer would have charm, but why was he
using it on her? After what had happened the other
afternoon, she was frankly surprised he was even civil
to her, let alone flattering.

Deliberately assuming an air of composure, Catherine stepped slightly back from him before saying, 'I
can't believe that's the reason you're asking me out.'
There was definite note of bewilderment in her voice
that she couldn't disguise.

'Well, not entirely,' he offered, and she looked at
him sharply, suddenly cautious. 'I wanted to make up
to you for my behaviour the other day. I'm afraid I was
rather rude to you when I left here and was hoping you
would let me apologise by taking you out to dinner.'

'B-but,' Catherine stammered in confusion, 'I
ruined your clothes.'

'And apologised very sweetly for the accident,' he

said smoothly. His lips pursed in a chagrined gesture. 'I wasn't very sweet to you, though, was I? I'm really quite ashamed of myself and hope you will overlook my rudeness. Please, won't you have dinner with me and let me show you I'm not always such a boor?'

His tone was warmly sincere, but Catherine met his eyes warily. She had resented the way he had rebuffed her attempts to apologise after the accident, but never in her wildest dreams had she imagined he would be ashamed of his behaviour.

She wasn't altogether sure she believed him now. She knew the type of women Kent Latimer dated, or at least those he sent flowers to: society types, the occasional model. Somehow, a florist with a small shop didn't fit the picture.

Curiosity warred with caution, as she weighed the pros and cons of going out with him. She supposed the worst that could happen would be that he would turn out to be an absolute drip and she would be bored all evening. Smiling suddenly, she remembered she wouldn't have to work on the books tonight, either.

'I'd be pleased to have dinner with you Mr Latimer,' Catherine accepted politely. The shock of his unexpected invitation had worn off and she was starting to look forward to the evening.

'Please call me Kent,' he replied silkily, then: 'I'll pick you up at your apartment about eight.' He reached down and took her hand, lifting it to his lips and gently placing his lips against the back of it. 'Until tonight, Cat,' he murmured softly, looking deep into her eyes, and then he was gone.

For several seconds Catherine stared dumbfounded at the shop door. She looked down at her hand and touched the spot where his lips had been. Kissing her hand like that had been so incredibly ... *corny*. So why hadn't she laughed in his face instead of gaping at him like some starry-eyed teenager? He certainly knew how to keep a girl off-balance, Catherine thought, wondering if she had made a mistake in agreeing to go out with him. She frowned and rubbed the back of her hand against her skirt, suddenly very wary of Kent Latimer.

As she went back to her office she avoided Paula's curious stare, unwilling to discuss her visitor with the girl. She needed to think. He hadn't asked for the address of her apartment, and now that she thought about it, he had called her Delaney and not used her stage name, Devlin. Obviously he had checked her out before asking her for a date. But why?

CHAPTER TWO

CATHERINE was aware of the curious stares that followed them as the maître d' led them to their table by the window—that the eyes of the other women in the room were faintly envious as they rested on her escort. And well they might be, she thought, glancing at the handsome profile of Kent Latimer. His reputation as a ladies' man was justly deserved, and although she knew she was foolish to succumb to his practised technique, she couldn't help being impressed by him.

He had arrived at her door promptly at eight, declining her invitation for a drink before they left. Instead, he had taken her to the revolving lounge on top of the Sheridan Landmark for pre-dinner cocktails. Over forty floors above the street, it gave a magnificent, three-hundred-and-sixty-degree view of the city, without it being necessary to turn one's head. Not that Catherine had really noticed the view, she was far too enthralled with her companion. Somehow Kent Latimer managed to combine an old-fashioned chivalry that made a woman feel cherished and protected with a modern regard for her opinions and ideas that afforded her respect and equality as a person. Throw in the fact that he was attractive, wealthy, undoubtedly sexy, and very eligible and it was no wonder she was half-way to finding him irresistible and their date had barely begun.

By the time they had left the Sheridan for the restaurant in another prestigious Vancouver hotel,

Catherine was in a state of heady well-being that had
nothing to do with the Martini she had consumed. Her
usual reserve towards men seemed to have deserted
her and she was determined to make the most of her
date with Kent. She was tired of lukewarm friendships
that never touched her emotions, and Kent Latimer
was the most interesting man she had met in years.
Allowing herself to become infatuated with him was
amusing.

When they reached the table, Kent held her chair
for her, making sure she was comfortably settled
before taking his own seat. He sent a warm smile to
her across the candlelit table before turning to accept
the wine list from the waiter. Kent gave it a cursory
glance, only ascertaining her preference for red or
white, before ordering an imported Chardonnay.
Then he turned his attention to the dinner menu,
occasionally making suggestions as to what Catherine
might like to eat.

The wine approved and poured, their order taken,
the last waiter glided away from the table, leaving
them alone. Kent took an appreciative sip of his wine,
then smiled across at Catherine. 'This is an excellent
wine. I hope you like it.'

Catherine sampled her own glass, quickly concealing her reaction. The wine was drier than she was used
to and tasted faintly astringent to her palate. 'Have
you eaten here before?' she asked, deciding wine was a
topic it might be best to avoid. When she had been a
singer, she hadn't drunk at all, it didn't fit with the
image she had tried to project, and in the years since
then she had had little opportunity to acquire the taste
for fine wines.

Kent nodded in answer to her question. 'They

usually do quite a good job of the meal, and the service is excellent.'

Catherine looked around and found another waiter watching them with predatory regard. 'They tend to make you feel almost guilty if you don't give them something to do,' she commented, laughing softly as the man leapt into action to light the cigarette of a woman seated at a nearby table.

He followed the direction of her gaze. 'I'm glad to see you don't smoke, it's not a habit I find attractive.' He turned back to her. 'But then you don't strike me as a person with vices.'

She swirled the pale gold wine in her glass, taking a small sip to hide her embarrassed flush. He seemed to be expecting some reply, so finally she said, 'Thank you for the compliment, but I assure you, I'm only human. I have my faults just like everyone else.'

He reached out and took her hand, his fingers twining in hers. Little lines of amusement fanned out from the corners of his eyes as he grinned at her. 'What are you hiding?' He chuckled softly, shaking his head. 'You have beautiful eyes—too beautiful to hide dark secrets.'

The waiter returned at that moment with their appetisers, and Kent released her hand to allow him to set the dishes before them. Catherine watched the man refill their wine-glasses, despite the fact that they had barely tasted the liquid. Kent's teasing comments had had a shattering effect on her mood. Dark secrets—why had he had to use that term? There were too many dark secrets in her past, secrets she could never tell anyone.

She bent her head to sample her appetiser, although the thought of food at that moment was repellent. The magic had gone out of the evening and she didn't know how to recapture it. Unaware of her withdrawal, Kent tasted his prawn cocktail, then took another sip of his wine before speaking. 'I hope you've forgiven me for my behaviour the other day,' he began, smiling at her. 'I wasn't being intentionally obtuse when I failed to recognise the name of Cat Devlin.'

For an instant the hand bearing a forkful of food to her mouth froze. What a fool she was! All the time she had been speculating on why Kent had asked her out, she had overlooked the most obvious reason of all.

Catherine forced herself to look up, to smile. Unfortunately for Kent Latimer, he was going to be disappointed; the last thing she would do was talk about her alter ego. *Cat Devlin.* 'You couldn't have been expected to, so there's nothing to forgive. Please, let's just forget about it.' She turned her attention back to her plate. 'This is quite good. I'm glad you recommended it.' She took a bite, The salmon tasted like cardboard.

'I'm glad you're enjoying it,' he echoed, then persisted, 'but Catherine, I'm really sorry about the way I acted that afternoon I came into your shop. I'm not normally that difficult to get along with, I assure you.'

'It isn't important, Kent,' she said, pushing her plate to one side. 'Besides, I wasn't exactly pleasant myself. I hope the person you gave the flowers to enjoyed them.'

'She did. They were for my secretary—a birthday gift. I happened to mention who you were and she turned out to be a great fan of yours.' He looked up to grin at her. 'The next morning she brought in this enormous scrapbook of press clippings about your career.' (A scrapbook—Catherine suppressed a grimace). 'You had an exciting life. I'm surprised you gave it up.' He paused, giving Catherine the opportunity of commenting, but when she remained silent, he continued, 'I suppose you didn't want to go on as a single after your brother died.'

'That's right.' How could she manage to introduce another topic of conversation without sounding rude?

'Losing your brother must have been a blow, especially as you'd lost your parents a few years earlier.' There was another of those pauses as he waited for her to speak, but what could she say? 'Your father was a minister, wasn't he? It couldn't have been easy to adapt to the life of a Las Vegas entertainer coming from that sort of sheltered background. You and your brother handled it well. A lot of kids your age would have been corrupted by that sort of life, though I suppose your parents still provided sound moral role models even though they had passed on.'

Catherine took a sip of her wine, finding it difficult to swallow and struggled with a half-hysterical urge to laugh. If Kent only knew! If she had followed her mother's role model she would have found it very easy to fit into the Las Vegas scene. In the ten years since Rick Moss, their manager, had concocted that phoney biography for her and Casey, Catherine was still amazed that they had never been found out.

Of course, if anyone was an expert at deception, it was Rick. He would have made a perfect camouflage officer for the army. Catherine bit her lip; she really didn't like thinking about Rick, about the secrets he kept. How could he and Brian have kept something like that from her? Rick, she could understand: getting help for Casey might have incurred publicity and he would have done nothing to jeopardise their career. But Brian—he was supposed to have been their friend!

For one frightening second, the image of Casey as she had last seen him filled her brain—his features relaxed in death, his body sprawled across the front seat of his car. Quickly she closed her eyes, pressing her hand to her forehead as if to push the image out of her mind forever. She wouldn't think about the Devlins, about Casey, about what had happened.

'Tell me, Cat,' Kent persisted, a touch of annoyance in his tone, 'what was it like being a successful entertainer?'

His question intruded into her thoughts and suddenly she was furiously angry. Looking up, she glared at him with a set face, and Kent's own mouth firmed. 'I imagine your life was quite different then,' he probed again, a stubborn light glinting in his eyes.

'It was,' Catherine said shortly.

'And you don't miss it?'

'No, I don't.' She focused on a point just beyond his shoulder. Did she miss it? Strangely enough she didn't know the answer. Sometimes she would recall the surge of adrenalin that had shot through her when she had stepped out on to the stage, the heady sensation that seemed to lift her right off her feet when the applause started. But singing—that had been only a small part of being Cat Devlin. As for the rest of it— she would *never* go back, and at the thought of it she found herself clenching her hands in her lap. The long hours, the pressure, the demands that had taken so much out of her that she had lost her brother even before his death.

Resentfully, Catherine met Kent's eyes, her own glacial. 'If you've read the clippings, there isn't anything I can add to them,' she said curtly.

The awkward silence that followed this statement was finally broken by the arrival of a waiter. He removed their used plates and topped up their wine-glasses before leaving them alone again, while Catherine fiddled nervously with her napkin. She knew she had angered Kent, but he had left her no way of avoiding it. Finally, as the lengthening silence became even more uncomfortable, the orchestra started to play a lively number with a strong Latin beat, and in desperation she asked, 'Do you think we could dance to this?'

Kent frowned slightly, but good manners dectated he should agree, and laying his napkin aside, he rose from his chair to escort her to the dance floor. As he led her through the steps of the rumba, Catherine looked up at him and smiled uncertainly, but he wasn't looking at her, his face set. She was guiltily aware she had handled things badly, but although she was a little ashamed of her churlishness, there had seemed no other way of choking him off.

Fortunately the waiter arrived with a trolley as soon as they returned to their table and further conversation was not instantly necessary. Assuming an interest she didn't feel, Catherine watched the waiter prepare their salad. He made a minor production of the process, tossing the ingredients together with exaggerated gestures and finally serving it with a theatrical flourish.

As soon as the man wheeled the cart out of range, Kent laughed softly. 'To be honest with you, I don't particularly like Caesar salad, but I always order it just to see him go through that routine.'

Catherine looked at him quickly to see that his warm, attractive smile had returned, and she felt the tension drain from her. He had forgiven her for her refusal to talk about her career. Her eyes glowed with happiness as they met his and she tackled her salad with renewed appetite.

As they sipped coffee and liqueurs later, Catherine decided she couldn't remember when she had enjoyed an evening so much. There had been that bad patch at the beginning of the meal, but since then it had been delightful. Kent was a fascinating personality, extremely well read and intelligent, and though Catherine's own education had been sketchy, he didn't try to make her feel inferior by talking down to her.

For a time, they discussed his political ambitions, and Catherine began to be caught up in his enthusiasm. Having gained experience in government at the local level, he planned to move into the arena of national politics in the near future, and as he discussed his ideas, Catherine found her admiration for him growing. While he had definite opinions on the issues, he was not dogmatic in his views and invited her comments and gave them due consideration.

They had finished their coffee and Kent was escorting her from the restaurant a few minutes later when he drew her over to a table near the entrance. 'Peter . . . Leanne! I didn't see you earlier. You could have joined us for coffee.'

The man sitting at the table arose smiling. Though about the same height as Kent, he was stockier, with very broad shoulders that owed nothing to the tailoring of his dinner jacket. 'We thought about it, but you two didn't look like you would welcome company.' His grey eyes twinkled as he saw Catherine blush.

'Very perceptive of you,' laughed Kent, slipping his arm around Catherine's waist and smiling down at her. 'Catherine, I'd like you to meet my tactful friend, Peter Castle, and this is his sister, Leanne. Peter, Leanne, this is Cat Devlin.'

Catherine started, and she felt Kent's arm about her waist tighten as he looked at her quickly. Why hadn't it occured to her that he would introduce her as Devlin and not Delaney? Peter held out his hand to shake hers, and it took her a moment to collect herself enough to offer her own. As her hand was engulfed in his, she could only hope that he wouldn't notice the faint trembling she couldn't control.

'Cat Devlin,' Peter repeated the name. 'This is a pleasure. I thought you looked faintly familiar. I saw you and your brother perform several years ago.' He released her hand and looked back at Kent. 'How about joining us for coffee? You've had this lovely lady to yourself for long enough.'

His sister echoed the invitation and Kent looked at Catherine enquiringly. Pointedly, she looked at her watch. She didn't want a replay of that earlier conversation with Peter and his sister. 'I really don't want to stay out too late, and I was looking forward to that walk you promised me . . .' She smiled at Kent, then turned to Peter. 'I'm sorry. Would you mind if we took a rain-check?' Like for about two hundred years from now.

Peter shrugged regretfully. 'I'll hold you to that . . . in fact . . .' he looked at Kent, 'is Cat coming to the benefit with you?'

'I haven't asked her yet, but I'm hoping she will.'

'Great, I'll take good care of her while you make your speech—that way she won't get bored.'

He winked at Catherine, but she didn't notice. Benefit . . . speech . . . there were bound to be reporters there. And with Kent as her escort, her presence would be news. 'When is this benefit?' she asked.

'Next weekend, Saturday actually,' Peter supplied.

'I'm afraid I couldn't possibly make it.' Catherine tried to look regretful as relief flooded her. 'I have a florist's shop and I'm contracted to do the flowers for two weddings the next day, so I'll have to work that evening. Perhaps some other time.'

'Couldn't your assistant fill in for you?' Kent interposed.

'She hasn't been with me very long,' Catherine replied. 'She doesn't have the experience to take over yet. I'm sorry, but I'll have to give it a miss.'

There was a brief silence, and finally Kent said, 'I understand.' Though he had accepted her excuse, his expression was faintly sceptical. 'Well, if we're going for that walk, we'd better move. I'll be seeing you, Peter, Leanne. So long.' He slipped his hand under her elbow to escort Catherine away.

'Would you like to come in for a nightcap?' Catherine asked a short while later. They had reached the door to the apartment and she was fumbling in her handbag for her key. Although she had been the one to say she didn't want a late evening, she was reluctant for it to end.

'I'd better not. I have an early appointment in the morning.' She found her key and Kent reached out and took it from her, unlocking her door.

Catherine stood uncertainly in the open doorway. 'Well, then . . . thank you for a lovely evening . . .' She stared up at him, her throat suddenly dry. She had been waiting hours for this moment when he would finally kiss her and now it looked as though he wasn't going to. Disappointment washed over her and she quickly turned away so he couldn't read her expression. 'Goodnight, Kent,' she said huskily, taking a step into her apartment.

'Catherine,' he said softly, turning her back to him with a hand on her shoulder. She looked up and read the amusement in his eyes, as he pulled her into his arms. 'You didn't think I was going to let you get away without even a kiss, did you?'

She stared up at him, her pulse beginning to pound, and her lips parted softly as his came down on hers. His mouth was warm and sensuous as it covered hers, moving in gentle exploration, just as she imagined it would be. A warm flush flooded through her, awakening pleasurable sensations throughout her body, as her arms slid around his neck and her lips moved in tune with his. His hands were warm through the thin material of her top and it was only with difficulty that she checked the urge to yield against him.

Slowly, as though reluctant, Kent set her away from him. 'I'd better be going,' he said softly. Catherine stared into his face, her eyes wide and luminous. Drawn, his mouth found hers again, tenderly at first, then deepening as he felt her respond. He pulled her firmly against him, pressing her breasts against the hard wall of his chest. She felt a tremor go through him and knew it echoed the one in herself.

Abruptly, he released her, stepping back to put a space between them. 'I really must go,' he said, his voice slightly unsteady. 'Goodnight, Cat.' Turning, he quickly walked away.

She watched his retreating back, feeling dazed and a little confused, for though she had wanted him to kiss her, she hadn't been prepared for the depth of her response. She had occasionally wondered if she were frigid, since she was normally inhibited in her reaction to the physical advances of men. While she enjoyed their kisses, she had never visualised carrying the relationship any further. She hadn't wanted Kent to stop though, and the knowledge thoroughly disconcerted her.

He turned back to look at her when he reached the end of the corridor. For a moment he stared at her, his face expressionless, then like a magician conjuring a rabbit, he suddenly produced that melting smile and her heart lurched. 'I'll phone you,' he called back to her, then turned the corner and was gone.

After entering her apartment, Catherine prepared for bed, before seating herself in front of the mirror. She felt restless and as she pulled a brush through her long auburn hair, she grimaced at the reflection in the mirror. With her hair free from the confines of the chignon she usually wore, her cheeks slightly flushed, she'd resurrected the way she'd looked as singer Cat Devlin. Kent's questioning about her time as Cat had been the flaw in an otherwise perfect evening. She hoped her curtness had succeeded in convincing him that she wouldn't discuss the past. Musing, she realised how distinctly she separated the two identities in her mind, as if Cat Devlin were nothing to do with her. Indeed, settled in her life as Catherine Delaney, she really felt that Cat Devlin was a stranger and didn't stop to consider that no one can dismiss a large part of their life without damage.

Standing up abruptly, she eyed the bed reproachfully, knowing that with the state of her thoughts she would be unlikely to find peace in it tonight, and on impulse, she turned away to walk into the living-room and over to her desk. Opening the bottom drawer, she took out a long-playing record album. She had an extensive record collection housed in the rack next to her stereo, but this album had never been part of it.

For several minutes, she simply stared at the record

jacket. Both she and her brother were featured on the cover, but it was his face she focused on. He had been a handsome young man, Catherine thought, staring at the portrait. Looking at his wavy, dark hair, she smiled faintly, remembering how he had cursed it. Even for the photo, he hadn't been able to completely tame the lock which insisted on falling across his forehead whenever he moved. Her eyes held the bright blue ones in the portrait, then moved to the slightly crooked smile that their female fans had loved. A faint sprinkling of freckles marked the bridge of his nose and his complexion glowed with health in the photograph.

Biting her lip, Catherine frowned down at the image of her brother. It had been taken only a few weeks before his death. It just didn't seem possible he could have been taking drugs then, but she couldn't dispute the evidence. Since the day he had died, she had lived with the knowledge that her brother had been a drug addict.

Going to the stereo, Catherine switched it on. As the first notes sounded, she settled on the sofa, closing her eyes. She seldom let herself think of the past, but the memories were crowding in on her tonight and wouldn't be dismissed. How exciting it had all been in the beginning! She could still recall the glowing praise given them, the prediction that the Devlins' star would rise high in the heavens. To audiences disgusted with lewd stage shows and comedians who relied on bathroom humour to get their laughs, the Devlins were a breath of clean northern air, something totally new in the jaded world of Nevada's gambling centres. On stage and off, they were a clean-cut, wholesome pair who lived by the old-fashioned values and morals thought lost in the tinselled glamour of show business.

She had thought the magic would never end, that after the struggles of their childhood, she and Casey had found paradise. It wasn't until the day Casey died that she discovered their paradise was as much an illusion as the idyllic childhood Rick had created for them.

That day, her first indication that something was wrong was when Casey had failed to show up for their morning rehearsal. With their next opening only a week away, they had had a lot of new material to go through, and Catherine had been furious. In a temper, she had stormed out of the rehearsal hall and driven to his apartment to find him. When she reached the apartment, Brian Collins, Casey's valet-cum-body-guard, told her he hadn't been there since the previous evening, and that he had just returned from trying to find him.

Catherine's anger had instantly dissolved in a surge of anxiety. Several months earlier Casey had bought a high-powered Porsche 930 Turbo and frequently took it for a drive in the desert in the early hours of the morning. Now the car was missing from its parking space.

She had insisted that they contact the Devlins' manager, Rick Moss. He had handled their career since its inception and if anyone would know how to handle Casey's disappearance, he would. When Rick reached Casey's apartment, he told her to go back to her rehearsal at the hotel and he and Brian would go out into the desert to see if they could find her brother. She remembered that she had wanted to call in the police, check the hospitals, but Rick wouldn't let her. Until they knew what had happened, they couldn't afford any publicity. Surprisingly, Brian had sided with Rick. Catherine knew Rick well enough to know that his interest in the Devlins was purely monetary, but Brian was genuinely fond of Casey and for a time, Catherine felt her anxiety lessen. Nonetheless, she refused to return to the hotel and had insisted they allow her to accompany them.

Oddly enough, it hadn't taken them long to find him. Later, Catherine had sometimes wondered if Rick hadn't known exactly where to look. On first seeing her brother's body, sprawled across the front seat of the car, she couldn't accept what had happened. A heroin overdose—it couldn't be true. Her brother wasn't a junkie, he didn't take drugs so he couldn't have overdosed. He just *couldn't*!

Even when Rick had shown her the paraphernalia of an addict in her brother's jacket pocket, she hadn't wanted to believe. Only when both he *and* Brian confessed that they had known for months that Casey was taking something did the truth sink in. Rick might lie about something like that for his own reasons, but she knew Brian could be trusted to tell her the truth. Nevertheless, she couldn't forgive either of them for keeping it from her until it was too late.

Her cheeks were wet when the faint clicking sound from the stereo intruded into her memories. Wiping her eyes with the back of her hand as she stood up, she replaced the album in the desk, closing the drawer with a decisive push. If only she had known, she might have been able to prevent her brother's destruction. Although she had agreed to the cover-up of his death, making it look like a car accident so her brother's image would remain untarnished, she knew that the Devlins' career had ended. The price of success had been too high.

CHAPTER THREE

THE next morning Catherine sat at her desk and stared dreamily at the door of her office. She really should get down to untangling the mess she had made of the calculations in the ledger that lay before her, but it was much more fun to sit and think about last night, about Kent. He had said he would call, but, she thought optimistically, he might drop in. His office was just upstairs; he wouldn't be going out of his way.

Sighing softly, she picked up her pen and looked down at the column of numbers in the book. Sales tax—who wanted to worry about sales tax? Still, she applied herself to the chore and was soon lost in a world of bewildering forms and calculations that left no room for other thoughts to intrude.

When the phone rang, she reached for it absentmindedly: seven per cent of—she tried to hang on to the thought as she spoke automatically into the mouthpiece. 'Dogwood Florist's.'

'Good morning, Cat,' Kent's low, faintly husky voice sounded in her ear and sent every number flying out of her head. 'Are you busy?'

Catherine looked down at her desk and wrinkled her nose. 'No,' she lied.

'Good. I didn't want to interrupt anything.'

'I wasn't doing anything important.' The tax man might not agree, but she didn't care.

'I was wondering if you were free tomorrow night?'

'Well,' she said cautiously, 'I'm not really sure. Er ... what were you thinking of doing?'

36

'The RCMP Musical Ride is at BC Place. My dad's company has a box and I thought you might enjoy going to see them.'

'Oh, I see,' Catherine hedged. It was an attractive offer: scarlet-coated Mounties performing a precision drill on horseback set to music. She admitted she was curious about the loge too: she had seen a piece on television about the box seats at the new stadium when it had first opened, and knew they were more like luxury suites than seats in an arena. She also knew they held a dozen or more people.

'Are you interested?' Kent asked, and Catherine realised how long she had been silent.

'Er . . . it sounds very nice, but I don't think you should count on my being able to make it.'

'You have other plans?' There was a rime of frost in his tone now and Catherine bit her lip.

'Well, not a date . . .' She fingered a page of her ledger, then gave a brittle laugh. 'In a way it is—with the tax man. I have to have my sales tax in on Monday and if I don't do it tomorrow night, I don't know when I'll get it done.'

'You can't get it done before then?' he pressed.

'I'll probably work on it, but . . . I'm not very good at bookkeeping, so I can't really plan on having it finished.'

'I see.' He paused. 'I would have thought you would have an accountant to handle that sort of thing for your shop.'

'I think it's better to keep track of the money in a business yourself.'

'But if you have difficulties with it, wouldn't it be better to hire a professional?'

'Not necessarily,' Catherine responded. 'I mean, at least I know I'm honest.'

'So are the vast majority of accountants,' Kent returned drily.

'I didn't mean to say they weren't,' she assured him hastily. 'It's . . . I don't know . . . you know what they say: once bitten, twice shy,' Catherine finished lamely.

'Oh, someone cheated you?' he asked with interest.

'Well . . . not really. I just don't think it's wise to give someone else control of your business affairs.' How did they get on to this topic? She wasn't going to explain about Rick. 'Anyway, Kent, I am sorry about tomorrow night, but I'm almost positive I'll have to work.'

There was a brief silence at the other end of the line, then Kent said in a stilted voice, 'I understand. I'm sorry. I think you would have enjoyed it.'

'I probably would have,' Catherine agreed softly. There was a short awkward silence and, at war with herself—she wanted to see him despite the risks—she knew he was going to say goodbye and hang up. Suddenly she blurted out, 'I'll be free Monday night . . . I did the flowers for a new restaurant on Hastings Street a few weeks ago and, at the time, I thought it sounded like a nice place to try. It serves Greek food.' She had spoken quickly and now she stopped and drew a deep breath. Women's Lib may have been around for years, but *she* had never asked a man for a date before. 'Would you have dinner with me there on Monday?'

She held her breath as she waited for him to answer.

'I would love to,' he responded, and she could breathe again.

'Oh, thank you.' She was unaware that he had heard the relief in her voice and had started to grin. She cleared her throat. 'Mmm . . . I don't have a car, so will it be OK if you meet me there?'

'Why don't you let me pick you up at your apartment?' he suggested, and then reading her next thought, added, 'And I'll be taking care of the bill, by the way.'

'I couldn't let you do that. I——'

'Don't argue ... I won't come otherwise.'

'Oh ... in that case ...'

'Fine. Seven o'clock at your apartment?'

'I'll see you then,' she agreed. She was still smiling long after she had gently replaced the receiver in its cradle.

'You look very lovely tonight, Cat,' Kent commented after the waiter left to fill their order.

'Thank you.' She smiled warmly at him, her eyes glowing in the candlelight. She was happy, happier than she could ever remember having been in her life before. She had been out to dinner often with Kent in the past month and every time she saw him, she fell a little more under his spell as he charmed her into forgetting her misgivings about being seen with him. It was only when she was alone that doubts surfaced. And these she refused to think about. Just as she refused to examine her own feelings towards him.

'Cat, I've something I want to ask you,' Kent said a moment later. 'Peter Castle is giving a small dinner party tomorrow night and I'd like you to accompany me.'

'Tomorrow night?' she asked cautiously, her smile flickering.

'That's right. It's mainly a social evening, though I can't guarantee that we won't talk some business. Some of the people who will be there are quite influential politically and I'll be trying to gain their

support for my candidacy in the next election,' he said
frankly, studying her intently. 'I want you to come
with me.'

'Tomorrow night?' Catherine repeated, stalling for
time. 'That isn't much notice . . . I really don't think I
can make it.'

'You're busy?' Kent asked sharply, his eyes narrowing, though she sensed he wasn't surprised by her
answer.

'Well, I'm very behind at the shop. I—I . . . the bills.
I have to send out the bills day after tomorrow. I'll
need to work on them tomorrow night.'

Catherine looked at Kent, trying to gauge how
effective her excuse had been. She saw a flash of
impatient anger cross his face and knew it hadn't been
very well received. Kent was growing more irritated as
time went on with her thinly veiled excuses for
refusing to be seen anywhere with him where they
might encounter the press or his friends. Her adamant
refusal to discuss the past didn't help matters, either.

'You never can make it, can you, Cat?' he said
softly, his voice terse with anger.

She attempted to divert him. 'I don't know what you
mean. I do have a business to run and I have to attend
to it.'

'Look, Cat,' he said abruptly, 'let's stop playing
games. I want to know what's going on.'

Catherine shook her head, knowing she was being
backed into a corner. 'I don't know what you're
talking about.'

'You know exactly what I'm talking about. This is
the third time I've asked you to accompany me
somewhere when we'll be with a group and every time
you've come up with some excuse. Why?'

'Has it occurred to you that maybe I'm just not

interested in standing around talking politics all night?' she asked defensively.

'Is that it? I don't think so. There's something else. I don't know what it is, but I sure as hell would like to. Last week, when we were having dinner and Todd Black the reporter walked in? I wanted to take you over to meet him and suddenly you developed a violent headache, so I had to take you home instead.' His eyes pinned hers.

'Are you saying I didn't have a headache? That I lied?'

'Well, did you? I get the distinct impression that you don't want anyone to know that you're Cat Devlin.'

Catherine knew she had paled and only hoped Kent wouldn't notice in the dim lighting. 'Don't be silly, Kent,' she prevaricated, forcing a light laugh past her tight throat. 'Whatever gave you that ridiculous idea?'

'Is it ridiculous?' he asked, studying her. 'That first time I saw you, I noticed you seemed angry with your friend Nancy when she told me who you were. At the time, I just thought maybe you were embarrassed because I walked in when you were singing.'

'Well, I was embarrassed,' Catherine seized on the excuse he had given her. 'I mean, my career as a singer is finished and I don't think it's necessary that everyone knows what I used to do for a living.'

'But is that all it is? When I introduced you to Peter Castle as Cat Devlin, you jumped about a foot. Since then, you've made darn good and sure I don't have the opportunity of introducing you to anyone else. Every time I ask you out, you give me the third degree before you'll accept!'

'I thought you understood why I can't accept every invitation you extend. My business doesn't run itself.

It's only natural that I'm sometimes too busy to go out with you.'

'It's not just that,' he continued stubbornly. 'Every time I bring up your former career, you choke me off. You've told me all about your business, your friends, but never your singing career or anything that happened before then, either. It's like you were born in that flower shop!'

'I don't like raking over the past.'

'Why?'

'Because I'm a florist now, not Cat Devlin the singer. I had that life, and I left it. People seem to think because you have a career on stage, they have a right to know everything that you do off stage. But I *don't* live in the limelight any more and now I can demand my right to privacy.' Catherine ran her hand over her forehead, before looking back at him. 'I loved my brother, but Casey's gone, he's dead. As far as I'm concerned, Cat died with him. I'm content with my life now: I don't want to dredge up what happened five years ago.'

Fortunately, the waiter arrived with their salads just then and they leaned back to allow him to serve them. For several minutes, they ate in tension-filled silence. Although the salad was delicious, Catherine had to force herself to eat it.

After a few minutes, Kent pushed his plate away. 'I can accept that you would prefer not to discuss your past, but that doesn't explain why you continually refuse to meet my friends or accompany me to any functions when there's a chance our relationship might be publicised.'

Catherine sighed unhappily, knowing she would have to give him some sort of explanation. Finally, she said, 'I don't accept your invitations because I know you'll introduce me as Cat Devlin. As soon as people find out who I am, they want to know all about my career, my brother, my whole life, and I'd rather avoid all that.'

'Are your memories of that time in your life so painful?'

'Yes, they are,' Catherine said flatly.

For several moments Kent remained silent, studying her. Nervously, Catherine toyed with her cutlery, wishing he would just drop the whole thing. He reached out his hand, covering hers as it fingered her spoon. 'Catherine, look at me,' he commanded gently, and she was compelled to look up at him. 'If your memories are painful, running away from them won't make them go away. You gave up a very successful career five years ago, but it didn't bring your brother back. Refusing to acknowledge that part of your life now isn't going to do it either. It isn't natural. It's time you came to terms with your past. Pretending the Devlins didn't exist doesn't solve anything.'

She gave her head a helpless little shake. 'You don't understand. I can't explain, but my past, my brother . . . it's better to just forget all that.'

'No, it isn't better,' he persisted. Catherine made a denying gesture and tried to extract her hand, but his grip tightened. 'I'm trying to help you get your life into perspective.'

'I'm perfectly happy with my life the way it is,' she asserted impatiently, managing to free her hand. 'I don't want to get it into "perspective".'

Irritation settled on his face, his lips drawing into a fine line. Finally he broke the silence. 'I'm going to put my cards on the table, Cat. I like you, I want to keep seeing you, but dammit, I have a lot of social commitments in my life. I need a woman at my side when I attend these affairs, and I want that woman to be you.'

Catherine remained silent, her emotions a curious mixture of misery and joy. Kent wanted her at his side, but how could she be there? If Rick ever found out he would hound her into finishing her contract with him. And that she could not face—not Rick, not performing, ever again. As far as she was concerned, as she had told Kent, Cat Devlin was dead. That way she did not have to face up to the pain of betrayal by those she had loved and trusted.

Kent studied her lowered head for several moments, then said softly, 'I thought you felt something for me, that we've been growing closer over the past few weeks.'

'I—I am fond of you, Kent,' Catherine replied. She looked up suddenly, smiling slightly. 'If I agreed to go to these places you want me to, couldn't you introduce me as Catherine Delaney?'

'Wouldn't that just be avoiding the issue, the way you've avoided it for five years?'

'You don't understand.'

'No, *you* don't understand. You are Cat Devlin,' he said forcefully. 'It's time you stopped pretending that you aren't.' When she stayed silent, looking away from him, he tried a different tack, 'You say you're fond of me. Haven't you ever considered how much you could help me?'

'What do you mean?'

Kent hesitated briefly, then said, 'The name of Cat Devlin is still remembered in this town. It would be good publicity for my career to have it known that I'm seeing you.'

'I . . . see,' Catherine said slowly, wishing she didn't. She felt the dull thump of her heart as his words penetrated her numbed mind. Suddenly the conversation had taken on a completely different complexion. It had been a long time since someone had dated her just because she was Cat Devlin, singer. It used to be an accepted part of her life, just as she had dated men she didn't particularly care for, because they were good for her image. But Kent she *had* cared for. She felt a coldness deep inside her as she began to take in how much she cared for him—despite the fact that he had just admitted he only saw her as a useful prop—a publicity stunt. Catherine concentrated on her wineglass, rolling the stem between her fingers, watching the pale liquid sparkle in the candlelight, as she realised just how often Kent called her Cat instead of Catherine. All the doubts she had refused to face rushed into her mind. She was being betrayed again. As much by her own delusions as by the man sitting opposite her. But it hurt.

Kent reached across the table and took her fingers. 'Do you, Cat?'

She neatly extracted her hand, giving him a cool smile that masked all feeling. 'I understand perfectly. You're far from the first man to take me out to further his image.' She took a swallow of wine, her throat dry.

He muttered something under his breath, then said, 'That isn't what I said. Try to understand. My political career is very important to me. I've invested a lot of myself in it, but so have others. I've had a lot of support from my family and friends. Wouldn't you like to make your contribution?'

'As Cat Devlin?'

'Yes,' Kent said firmly. 'It will do you as much good as it will me. If the past is painful for you, you should face it.'

Catherine studied him intently, her hurt turned to

anger. 'You hypocritical bastard! You must think I'm a complete fool. You couldn't care less about me, whether I "get my life into perspective". All you want is to trade on the name of Cat Devlin. Unfortunately, Mr Latimer, I don't intend to let you. I can see absolutely no benefit to be derived from continuing to see you,' she said contemptuously.

Dark crimson crept up his face as a muscle in his jaw twitched. Catherine saw him clench his fist and she unconsciously moved back in her chair. For all his charm, Kent had a well-defined streak of arrogance in his make-up. She had been deliberately insulting, and Kent wasn't a man to take kindly to insults. Suddenly he smiled—if the cruel twist of his lips could be called a smile. His eyes mocked her as he said, 'Can't you? I got the impression that you enjoyed our ... love-making,' he jeered.

Catherine blanched, hating him for bringing that up. She had been helpless to mask her response to his touch. That their physical relationship had been confined to kisses and light petting was due only to his restraint and not hers. She thought he respected her, wanted to—— Digging her nails into the palms of her hands, she felt she had never been angrier with herself. Somewhere in the back of her mind, she realised she had been expecting him to ask her to *marry* him ... that he was waiting for their *wedding night*. Fool! Just how far had she deluded herself?

She glanced up at the man sitting across the table from her, noting the arrogant set of his jaw, the faintly cynical expression in his eyes. She blanched as the truth hit her. She was in love with him! Frantically she told herself it was only infatuation—purely and simply physical attraction. She held on to that thought as she took a deep anguished breath to help pull herself together. She lowered her eyes and when she looked up again, her face was composed.

'Perhaps I'm as good at acting as you are, Kent. Why shouldn't I have pretended to enjoy your mauling?' she said smoothly. 'City aldermen do have a certain amount of influence. It can be very useful having one on your side if you're in business.' She gave him a tight little smile.

'So there is a benefit in seeing me,' he said softly.

She saw then how careless her remarks had been. She quickly shook her head. 'Not any longer, Kent. Unfortunately, it hasn't worked out. You see, I've realised that you aren't quite as helpful as I thought.'

'Ah . . . but I haven't really been trying to help you.' He smiled with satisfaction. 'I can, you know. That flower shop means a lot to you, doesn't it? I could do a lot to help you. As you say, I have influence. Many of the people I'll be introducing you to are just the sort of clients you want. They buy a lot of flowers. Who knows, you might even find you're so successful you want to open another shop, or expand. Aldermen can be very helpful in cutting through the red tape of business licences and building permits.'

'I've managed to do quite well on my own. I don't think I need your help.'

He looked at her and laughed. 'Darling, you have a lovely little shop, but I doubt it does little more than pay the bills at this point.' His eyes swept over her dress, and she knew he was assessing its cost. Granted, it wasn't a designer creation, but her temper rose as he dismissed it as being cheap. 'Don't tell me you've forgotten what it's like to be seen in the right places, to dress in the right clothes. I'll buy you a roomful of clothes if you like. And jewellery.' His smile grew slightly condescending as they rested on the pearls at her throat and she suddenly realised he assumed they were fake. For some reason, she felt upset. The pearls and the other jewellery she had retained from her years as a singer would realise a small fortune if she cared to sell them. She was hardly a candidate for the poorhouse, as he seemed to be implying.

'You were a celebrity, you can't tell me you never miss it,' he continued on a slightly different tack before she could find the words to counter him. 'In fact, you might even decide you want to resume your career once you get over this fixation you have against people knowing who you are.'

'That's where you're wrong,' Catherine asserted, annoyed at his constant misreading. 'I'll never sing professionally again.'

'I didn't say you have to,' Kent assured her, eyeing her curiously. 'I enjoy going out with you, I enjoy your company. But, Cat, you won't let me take you anywhere but out to dinner for just the two of us. My career demands I lead a little more varied social life than that. I want to include you in that social life, that's all. In exchange, I'll do what I can to help your business.'

She took a deep breath. He made it sound so simple, so reasonable. He just couldn't understand how much he was asking of her and she couldn't tell him. She sat in silence, studying Kent thoughtfully. In the flickering candlelight, his face was relaxed, only his eyes betraying that he was waiting for an answer. Although she found the prospect of reassuming her identity as Cat Devlin upsetting, she was wavering. She knew with certainty that if she refused his request, she would never see him again. And she couldn't face that. Yet she would be an absolute fool to continue seeing him.

But she couldn't silence a small voice within her. If she went along with him, what harm would they be doing anyone? It was not as if she disagreed with his political philosophy. She certainly wouldn't be the first entertainer to lend support to a politician. As long as she didn't sing, Rick could have no hold over her. It wasn't likely that he would even find out that she was seeing Kent—Vancouver was a long way from Las Vegas. Besides, it was possible that she would cure her infatuation for Kent faster by continuing to see him than by cutting him out of her life altogether. And then she could drop back into obscurity again, with no one any the wiser. She'd done it before, she could do it again.

'Cat, is what I'm asking such a hardship?' Kent asked softly. 'Surely after all these years you should be able to handle a few questions about your singing career?' He reached across the table and took her hand. Standing up, he pulled her to her feet. 'Dance with me. We'll talk later.'

Reaching the dance floor, Kent swung her easily into his embrace. Gradually she found herself relaxing, enjoying the feel of being in his arms. The orchestra was playing a moody Barry Manilow number and Kent pulled her closer. The wine earlier, the soft music, the spicy scent of his aftershave were weaving a spell around her. She leaned her head against his chest, resting it in the hollow just below his shoulder. Her hair stirred slightly as his lips brushed it gently. She suddenly felt close to tears.

The music ended and the orchestra announced that they would be taking a break. Meekly, Catherine followed Kent back to the table, wishing they did not have to continue their conversation. He helped her into her chair, then returned to his own. 'We dance

well together, Cat,' he murmured. 'We could do a lot
of things well together. Will you do as I ask?' he went
on, his persistence wearing her down.

'I'll let you introduce me to your friends, Kent. But
don't ask me to appear professionally, because I won't
do it. Understand?' He nodded, then gave her an
encouraging smile. With a sinking sensation she
wondered just what she had let herself in for. Did she
really think she would get over him by continuing to
see him, or was it simply that she couldn't bear the
thought of letting him go?

For pride's sake, Catherine pretended to enjoy the
remainder of the evening with Kent, although
depression wrapped round her like a shroud. Having
gained her agreement to his plans, he seemed content
to allow the subject to drop, much to her relief. But she
was inordinately thankful when they finally left the
restaurant and Kent escorted her to his car to take her
home. Neither of them spoke on the journey, and
within a few minutes they had arrived at her
apartment.

After switching off the engine, Kent shifted in his
seat as though to get out. Hurriedly Catherine said,
'Don't bother seeing me in.' She wanted desperately to
be alone. She reached down and fumbled with the
door handle, flinching in startled reaction when
Kent's arm came across to stop her. It brushed against
her breasts with intimate pressure and she shrank
back against the seat.

'Aren't you going to invite me in for coffee?' His
expression was unreadable in the dim glow from the
street lamps, but she sensed his surprise.

Her nerves were strung out like high tension wires
and they started to snap. He wanted to *use* her, trade
on her name to help his career, and suddenly, anger

blazed. He wanted to make love to her as though nothing had changed! Perhaps it hadn't for him but for her—— His arm was resting across her, his hand on her thigh, and abruptly, she knocked it away. 'No, I'm not. We made an agreement tonight. You're going to help me with my business and I'll help you with your career. It's a business arrangement, coffee isn't part of it.'

Kent leaned back in his seat, his eyes watchful. Catherine tried to steady her breathing. 'I thought you understood,' he said presently, impatience evident in his tone. 'Just because we've agreed to help one another, it doesn't mean we're not friends any more.'

'You stopped being my friend when you insisted I be Cat Devlin,' Catherine said, reaching down to find the door handle. 'I said I would do it, but that doesn't mean I have to like it—or you.'

Kent made an irritated sound in his throat, and Catherine knew she had angered him. Suddenly Kent's arms were on her shoulders, roughly turning her to face him. 'I am your friend, whether you believe it or not. You *are* Cat Devlin, and it's about time somebody made you face it. For five years you've been wallowing in self-pity because your brother died. Well, lots of people lose someone they love. It's about time you stopped playing the role of the self-exiled martyr and grew up.' His eyes glimmered dangerously in a mask of anger, then his mouth came down on hers, brutally crushing her lips. It was a kiss designed to punish, to hurt. The pressure forced her head back until her neck felt as though it would snap. She tried to struggle free, but the hard steel bands of his arms kept her firmly in check.

Finally she gave in and passively submitted to him. Sensing her weakening, Kent eased the pressure on her lips but did not end the contact. Treacherously her blood began to warm. Desire flickered, then flamed within her, betraying her will. His mouth moved gently over hers, coaxing and seductive, his tongue teasing her lips until they parted in unwilling surrender. Kent lifted his head and stared down at her, his face grim as he took in her dazed expression, her brown eyes softly luminous with awakened desire.

Hot colour flooded her cheeks as she tried to break away. He held her closely in his embrace, and she spluttered, 'Let me go!' Her eyes, black with hostility, clashed with his in the dimly lit car. 'The deal's off!'

He held her gaze for a moment, and when his arms slackened their hold, Catherine jerked away from him. Wrenching the door open, she scrambled out on to the pavement and turned to glare at him. 'Goodbye, Mr Latimer. Forgive me if I don't say it's been a pleasure knowing you.'

'Wait, Cat!' he called to her as she turned to stalk away. She heard his door slam and he came around the front of the car. He crossed to her, determination written in every line of his face. He grasped her upper arms in a firm but gentle grip, his eyes capturing hers in a steady gaze. 'I know I behaved badly just now. I shouldn't have lost my temper like that. I'll make it up to you . . . I promise. I won't touch you again unless you want me to.' His hands dropped to his side. 'Please . . . come with me tomorrow night?'

She had to tip her head back to look up at him. His face was gilded with the sulphur glow of the street light, his hair rumpled with one lock falling across his forehead stirring memories of Casey. Damn Kent, she cursed him. 'You'll leave me alone?' she asked crossly.

'I promise, Cat.'

'And you'll stop prying into my life as Cat Devlin?'

He nodded after a slight hesitation and she capitulated. 'OK.' Before she could change her mind, he left her. She stood watching as he got back into the car and started the engine, then turned slowly towards the entrance to her apartment as he drove away.

She had been genuinely fond of Nancy, but when the girl had probed too insistently into the past, Catherine had let her go out of her life with regret but also resignation. Why couldn't she let Kent go as well? Unable to delude herself any longer, she knew she had the answer to that question. She just wished she had the answer to why she had let herself fall in love with him.

CHAPTER FOUR

THE view had been one of the main factors in Kent's decision to locate his office in this room. On clear days, he could look out over Stanley Park and could almost forget he worked in the downtown area of a major city. At other times he would watch the freight traffic moving up Burrard Inlet for hours while he came to terms with some problem. If he worked late, he could look out and see the lights from the ski-lift on Grouse Mountain, strung out like a rope of diamonds against he black velvet of the mountain.

This morning Kent could find no comfort in the view. It was a damp drizzly November day, and fog pressed against the expanse of windows like thick cotton wool. However, he stared out at it, ignoring the legal brief lying open on the desk behind him, while he pondered the problem of Cat Devlin. He supposed he should be pleased that he had finally got her to agree to meet his friends, the first step in his plan for enlisting her help with his political campaign, but their argument last night had left a bitter taste in his mouth.

He had a successful law practice, was one of the youngest men ever elected alderman in Vancouver's history, and had a bright future in national politics. He had not got where he was today by misreading people, but he had made a serious error last evening. In the month he had been seeing her, he had waged a subtle campaign. Choosing his words carefully, he had gained her interest and finally her enthusiasm for his career ambitions.

During that time, he had also become aware that she was almost neurotic about concealing her identity as Cat Devlin, but had thought it a problem easily overcome. They would discuss her past, bring everything out into the open and then he would play his ace. He was aware of her feelings for him. Maybe she wasn't in love with him, but she was emotionally involved. He would use those tender feelings to gain her co-operation. What woman could resist an appeal for help from the man she desired?

In an angry gesture, he beat his fist against the arm of his chair. Nothing had gone as planned. She had frozen out his questions about her life as Cat Devlin, her reasons for abandoning her singing career. He knew little more about her now than before.

Finally in frustration he had moved on to the second stage of his campaign to win her co-operation. Kent frowned. Had he been wrong about how she felt about him? Though she had admitted her fondness for him, later she had insisted their relationship was solely a business one and that she had been seeing him only in hopes of benefiting her florist's shop, though he wasn't too sure if she meant that or whether it had simply been a defence. And if she were emotionally attached to him, wouldn't she have seen his point of view? Surely she must realise that a man in his position couldn't afford to conduct his social life out of the public eye? People were curious about him, it was only natural. If he wanted to represent them, they had a right to know about his private life.

He was almost relieved when the office intercom buzzed, interrupting his thoughts. Swivelling in his chair, Kent reached over and answered it.

'Mr Latimer, Mr Castle is here to see you.' His secretary's voice sounded faintly metallic as it came to him through the speaker.

'Good, send him in and bring us some coffee, please. Then you can take care of that little errand for me,' Kent said. As he waited for Peter, he smiled slightly, thinking of Miss Hamilton's errand. Cat's suggestion that they had a business agreement and nothing more had infuriated him last night. He didn't like feeling he had to resort to buying someone's support. This morning, though, he had decided to use it to his advantage. He would play the game by her rules, but he was going to make certain she was under an obligation to him so she couldn't change her mind.

The door to his office opened and Kent stood up to greet his friend, waving him into a chair. While they waited for Miss Hamilton to bring their coffee, they discussed the appalling weather and wondered if they would have to wait for spring before they finally saw the sun again. The coffee arrived and when the door closed behind the secretary, Peter opened his briefcase and removed a file folder.

'We're pretty well set for tonight,' said Peter, scanning a sheet of paper he had taken from the file. 'Gault's coming, as well as Simpson and Stokes. Concentrate on Gault—the other two will follow his lead, so he's the one you want to impress.' He looked up, smiling. 'He's interested already, so it shouldn't be too difficult. His support will be valuable.' He paused a moment, then asked, 'By the way, who are you bringing?'

'Cat.'

Peter's eyebrows lifted. 'Really? How did you manage that? I thought . . .'

'It wasn't easy,' Kent said grimly, turning his chair to stare out of the mist-shrouded windows. 'Do me a favour, Peter. Tonight, sit next to her, try to pump her.

I run up against a stone wall every time I question her about her career. See if you can figure out why she's so paranoid about talking about it.'

'Do you think I'll get any further than you have?'

'Well, I'm not getting anywhere,' shrugged Kent, then grimaced.

'You convinced her to come tonight,' Peter reminded him.

Kent swung back around, his expression angry. 'Only after I twisted her arm. I can't figure her out. I've read every bit of information I could find on her and there's nothing to explain this attitude of hers. She *says* she quit because her brother died, but it's got to be more than that. I know the press crucified her because she didn't go to his funeral, but that seems to have been more as a result of her avoidance of publicity than a reason for it.'

A brooding look replaced the anger in his face, and Peter sat silently watching his friend. Finally he suggested, 'Could it be she feels responsible for her brother's death?'

Immediately Kent shook his head. 'I don't see how. It was a car accident. Admittedly, it was pretty gruesome, the car burned and there wasn't much of a body left to recover, but it was definitely an accident. A pin from the steering mechanism had fallen out and he went over a cliff. How could she blame herself for that?' Kent paused for several moments, then said, 'I could see it if they'd been like most entertainers. Cat's pretty strait-laced and she wouldn't fit into the wild life of parties and dope and free love a lot of show business types go for, but the Devlins never did any of that. Hell, they were so pure they made the Osmonds sound like moral degenerates!'

He fell silent and went back to staring morosely out

into the fog. At last Peter said, 'I think you should drop her.' Kent turned to face him, his expression startled. 'She sounds like she has a lot of hang-ups, which is too bad, but to be honest, Kent, you're really not in a a position where you can afford to play amateur psychiatrist. Things are just starting to move for you. We can probably get you on the ticket for a by-election and, quite frankly, you should have your mind on that.' As he saw Kent's mouth press into a firm line, he smiled wryly and shrugged. 'Look, you've asked me to work with you on your political campaign, you pay me to advise you. That's what I'm doing. Forget Cat Devlin.'

'She could be a lot of help.'

'Who are you trying to convince, Kent? She hasn't sung professionally for five years and the public has nearly forgotten her. You have to coerce her into attending a simple dinner party. She's not willing to co-operate.' Peter saw the other man's jaw line harden but plunged on nevertheless. 'What's going to happen when the by-election is called? It's going to be one public appearance after another. If you're still involved with her then, she has to be at your side. Do you think she'll do it willingly?'

'She'll be used to it by then,' Kent said stubbornly.

'Will she?' Peter asked dubiously. When Kent ignored the question, he continued, 'OK then, what about your father?'

'What about him?'

'He's going to throw a fit when he finds out you're dating her. His support in this campaign is important too. You can't afford to alienate him.'

'My father would be the first to acknowledge the value of someone with Cat's renown supporting me. Besides, it's none of his business whom I date.'

'I think you want a little more from Cat Devlin than just political support or a few dates, though. But I also think you're living in a fool's paradise if you think James Latimer is going to accept Cat Devlin as his daughter-in-law without a murmur.'

'I never said I planned to marry Cat,' protested Kent, looking startled.

Peter met his eyes. 'Then why won't you give her up?'

'Because I think she'll be useful in my campaign,' Kent maintained.

'You're not in love with her?'

'I am not in love with her,' Kent stated firmly, but Peter couldn't help noticing he didn't quite meet his eyes as he said it. 'I pay you for your advice, but I make my own decisions. I think Cat Devlin is an asset. She can help me—you'll see tonight.' He stood up abruptly. 'Now, if you haven't anything more to discuss, I have this brief to get through.' He gestured to the papers on his desk.

Peter rose, accepting the dismissal. 'Of course. I'll see you tonight.'

After showing Peter out, Kent returned to his desk and picked up the top paper from the file. '"Whereas the party of the first part . . ."' He threw the paper back to the desk. Folding his arms behind his head, he stared up at the ceiling. He felt angry with Peter, angry with Cat—mostly with Cat. If she had co-operated, Peter wouldn't have any basis for jumping to such a wild conclusion. Peter just didn't realise how much Cat Devlin had to offer. She had been a big star and people *hadn't* forgotten her. And that was the *only* reason he wanted her at his side.

Shaking drops of rain from her umbrella as she

walked, Catherine hurried into the Grace Building.
Thank goodness for Paula! After Kent had left her last
night, it had taken her hours to fall asleep and as a
result she had slept through her alarm this morning,
but at least Paula had a key to the shop and would
have opened for her.

She pushed open the door to Dogwood Florist's and
went in. As always, she paused a moment upon
entering, sniffing delightedly at the fragrances that
lingered in the air. It was one of the things she enjoyed
most about owning a florist's. Even when it poured
with rain for days on end as it seemed to all winter,
Catherine always felt it was summer in the shop and it
lifted her spirits.

Shedding her raincoat, Catherine made her way to
the rear of the shop, pausing once to pull off a spent
bud from one of the hibiscus plants. Paula was
standing behind the service counter watching another
woman who was casually inspecting the display of silk
flower arrangements set up nearby.

'Sorry I'm so late, Paula,' Catherine apologised. 'I
slept through my alarm this morning. Have you had
any problems?'

The other girl shook her head. 'We haven't been
busy, but this lady has been waiting to talk to you.' She
indicated the middle-aged woman who had been
examining the display.

'Hello.' The woman stuck out her hand to shake
Catherine's. 'I can't tell you how delighted I am to
finally meet you, Miss Devlin.' She smiled cheerfully.
Catherine started slightly at the name, aware that
Paula was frowning curiously. 'I'm Mr Latimer's
secretary, Marjorie Hamilton. I feel like I've known
you for years, what with talking to you on the phone
and following your career.' Her assistant knew

nothing about her former occupation and was no doubt wondering how someone 'followed' the career of a florist.

'Perhaps we can talk in my office,' Catherine suggested quickly, indicating the door behind the counter. It was unrealistic to suppose she wouldn't have to come up with something to satisfy Paula's curiosity, but the less she heard now the better.

'Certainly,' Miss Hamilton agreed, and followed her into the office.

Closing the door behind them, Catherine indicated a chair and asked if her visitor would care for coffee. She agreed, and Catherine turned away to get some. She kept an automatic coffee-maker in her office and was glad to see that Paula had made the coffee earlier. Pouring out two mugs, she turned to ask Miss Hamilton how she took it.

'Black's fine,' the other woman answered. She was staring at the crumpled wads of paper littering Catherine's desk. Catherine felt slightly embarrassed. Kent's secretary looked very capable and undoubtedly wouldn't need several tries at filling in the forms necessary to running a business before she got them right.

'Now, for the reason Mr Latimer asked me to call on you,' Miss Hamilton said pleasantly as Catherine took her seat. For an awful moment Catherine wondered if he had sent her to take over the office work so she couldn't use it as an excuse for avoiding certain dates any longer, but dismissed the idea as the older woman opened her bag and withdrew a slip of paper. 'Mr Latimer wants you to have a new wardrobe,' the older woman said briskly. 'Here's a list of the things he thinks you need, as well as the stores where he has accounts so that you can charge them to him. He also asked me to give you his bank card, so if you find something you like somewhere else, it won't be a problem.' She handed Catherine the paper.

Catherine had been listening to the secretary with dawning horror, and as she read through the list, her colour mounted to a crimson: evening gowns, day dresses, riding wear, shoes and handbags, *lingerie*! She looked up at the woman incredulously. After his remarks last night, she wasn't altogether surprised that he wanted her to do something about her clothes. Yet it had never crossed her mind that he had really intended to buy her a complete new wardrobe. Catherine glanced up to see the woman watching her, her face burning with anger and embarrassment. Although the secretary's face was impassive, Catherine could imagine what she was thinking—that she was Kent's mistress. How could he be so insensitive as to put her in this position?

'He . . .' Catherine had to stop to clear her throat. 'He wants me to have these things?'

Miss Hamilton smiled matter-of-factly, causing Catherine to wonder just how many times she had been called upon to perform such a mission. 'Mr Latimer understands how busy you are but would like you to get started with the shopping as soon as possible.'

Catherine saw the loophole and dived through it like a rabbit down a bolthole. 'Well, this list is quite long, I can't possibly take any time off for shopping. I'm just too busy with my store.'

Miss Hamilton's reaction to this statement was a chuckle. 'Oh, he knows you quite well, doesn't he?' She beamed at Catherine indulgently. 'That's exactly what he said you'd say. That's why he sent me down here. I'm to catch up on your paperwork so you'll have time to shop.'

I was right! Catherine thought, gaping at the older woman. Before she could find her tongue to say anything though Miss Hamilton said quickly, 'You needn't look so worried. I'm quite familiar with this type of work. Before Mr Latimer employed me, I did freelance bookkeeping for several retail businesses. I won't have any trouble setting this to rights.' She looked at the desk, a confident expression lighting her rather plain features.

'I don't think . . .' Before Catherine could even start telling the woman what she didn't think, Miss Hamilton was sorting through the rubbish on the desk and Catherine was standing outside her shop, a hard plastic bank card bearing Kent Latimer's name in one hand and the list of items he considered essential additons to her wardrobe in the other.

Her fist clenched around the piece of paper, crumpling it, as she turned to march through the lobby and over to the elevator that would take her up to Kent's office. She took a step, then stopped and looked down at the credit card. So Kent Latimer thought she wore cheap clothes, did he? Well, maybe she should just let him see how expensive her tastes could be when she was in the mood! Buoyed up on a heady tide of revenge, she turned on her heel and strode quickly out of the building.

After slipping on her dress that evening, Catherine inspected her appearance in the full-length mirror. Cut from a shimmery teal-blue jersey, the gown fell from the strapless bodice into a delightful swirl at her feet. On the way, it clung lovingly to her curves, emphasising her firm bust and narrow waist. But the best part of all was that its price could easily have been mistaken for that of a good used car.

If ever a dress was made for diamonds, this one was it, she decided. Going to her jewellery box, Catherine took out her diamond set. The earrings were dainty tear-drops that matched the two-carat pendant that hung from a platinum chain. She slipped the matching bracelet on her wrist, a narrow band of platinum set with diamonds. Her hair was wound into a knot at the nape of her neck and as she tilted her head, the diamonds on her ears sparkled in the reflection.

The doorbell rang and, gathering up the white velvet cape she had bought that afternoon, she went to answer it. She opened the door to find Kent waiting for her, looking devastatingly handsome in a formal dinner jacket with a white ruffled shirt.

He didn't bat an eyelid when she handed him the receipts from her day's shopping, and disappointment put her in an aggressive mood.

'Well, do I meet with your approval?' asked Catherine shortly.

His mouth firmed as he reacted to the enmity in her tone, and he continued to study her. She saw his chin set at a belligerent angle, his eyes were glacial as he ran them over the dress. Finally he said in a flat voice, 'You look lovely.'

'I'm glad you approve,' Catherine accepted the compliment, her voice laced with sarcasm. 'I'd like to think you're getting your money's worth out of our deal.' She saw him flinch and knew she had touched a nerve. Taunting him, she lifted her chin. Maybe he hadn't been as unaffected by those bills as she had thought.

He continued studying her for a moment, then

asked, 'Why do you always wear your hair up like that?'

'I like it this way,' Catherine said with icy rudeness.

She saw the muscles of his jaw tense as he gritted his teeth in an attempt to control his temper. She was being deliberately antagonistic, but she didn't care. Her eyes glinted up at him challengingly. For a moment she thought he wasn't going to react, but when a slight smile of satisfaction started to form on her lips, he said abruptly, 'I don't. Wear it loose.'

She ignored the order, haughtily turning her back to him, and he took a step forward. 'Don't turn your back on me, Cat,' he ordered harshly. His hand snaked out and grasped her wrist, his other hand going to the back of her head and he began pulling out the hairpins that secured her hair. When Catherine tried to struggle away from him, he used her arm to lever her closer to him, forcing her body against him.

The intimate contact drove the air from her lungs in a gasp. She averted her head, aware that he was looking down at her and noting the colour inching up her cheeks. Her heart was beating wildly in her chest and when he shifted his stance slightly to slide his leg between hers, she capitulated. 'I—I'll take it down,' she choked out, and he released her immediately. Unable to bear the mocking amusement in his eyes a moment longer, she stalked into her bedroom, pulling out the few pins that still remained. Angrily, she tugged a brush through her long auburn tresses, wincing when a tangle caught in the brush and pulled her scalp. At that, she forced herself to calm down, though she was still fuming when she returned to the living-room.

'That's better,' Kent nodded. His eyes rested on the diamond pendant nestled against the creamy flesh of her neck. His fingers brushed against her skin as he lifted it to study it. The diamond glittered against the bronze tan of his hand, breaking the light into rainbows. 'Is this real?'

'Of course—but don't worry. You didn't pay for it. I've owned it for several years.' And even though she hated herself for bragging childishly, she added, 'I have a lot of nice jewellery and most of it's real, including the pearls.' As she stepped away from him, the diamond dropped back against her throat. 'Are you ready to leave?'

He took her cape, and she turned away from him so she could place it on her shoulders. His hands lingered on the cool flesh of her nape as he lifted her hair free from the wrap. 'Cat, are you saying those pearls and the other jewellery I've seen you wear aren't imitation?' he asked half-angrily, turning her to face him.

'What of it?' Catherine retorted.

'I see,' he said tightly. His mouth was set in a harsh line, his eyes cold.

'Just exactly what are you getting at?'

'Never mind. It's time we were leaving.'

'Not until you answer me,' Catherine dug her heels in as the implication of his remark sunk in. 'You think some man bought them for me, don't you?'

'Of course not. I didn't say that. Let's just drop the subject, shall we?' He went to the door and opened it, then turned back to her. 'Are you coming?'

'No. You have a mind like a sewer, Kent, and I'm not going out with you.' She crossed her arms in front of her, glaring at him.

'Yes, you are.' He stalked over to her, his hand taking her wrist in a hard grip. 'You're the one who said we had a *business* deal, and now I'm holding you to it. I've bought your company tonight with that dress you're wearing, my part of the *deal*.' He jerked her arm, pulling her to the door with him.

'Turn me loose, I'm not going anywhere with you!' Catherine struggled against him, twisting her arm to free herself. His grip was cruel, biting into the soft flesh of her wrist with bruising force.

At the door, he stopped suddenly. 'You are coming with me, and what's more, you'll behave yourself. Let me put it in language you'll understand. It's costing me a lot of money setting you up as Cat Devlin. We made a deal, and you're going to stick to it.'

'And just how do you think you're going to make me?'

He smiled then, an ugly twist of his lips that made her grow cold. 'Have you ever wondered why my law office is in the Grace Building? Let me tell you. It's because I happen to be one of the owners. Now I'm sure if we had a tenant I wasn't too happy with, I would have little problem getting them out. Have you got my meaning?'

'I have a lease.' Catherine glared at him defiantly.

'And I'm a lawyer and know all about breaking leases.'

Catherine opened her mouth, then snapped it shut. Regardless of his opinion of her, she knew she would have to go with him. She had built her whole life around that shop, she didn't want to lose it. 'I'll come,' she whispered. Kent dropped her wrist, and her hand tingled as the circulation returned. Already, a purple bruise was forming where his fingers had gripped her.

'I knew you'd see things my way,' he said imperiously, taking her elbow to lead her down the hall.

The cream Mercedes came to a halt in front of the

luxury apartment building. Kent got out and walked
around the bonnet to open the door for Catherine. He
helped her out, and pocketing his car keys, escorted
her into the lobby.

The drive had been accomplished in total silence
and much of Catherine's anger with Kent had
dissipated under a feeling of sick apprehension. As
they crossed the marble-tiled lobby, her stomach
muscles contracted into a hard knot, making it
difficult even to breathe. Until now, she had avoided
thinking about being introduced to a room full of
people as Cat Devlin, but in only a few seconds that
was exactly what would happen.

'Stop it, Cat,' Kent enjoined as the doors to the
elevator that would carry them to the penthouse
whispered shut. His eyes moved over her, suddenly
growing puzzled. 'What's the matter? You look like
you're about to pass out.'

'I'm fine,' Catherine choked out, hiding her
trembling hands in the folds of her cape. How could
she explain that the idea of meeting all those people as
Cat Devlin left her sick with fear? What if they had
heard rumours, what if they asked her about Casey?
She couldn't afford to make one mistake, one slip.

Kent stood facing her, frowning deeply as he noted
the pallor of her cheeks, the wide, hunted look in her
eyes. 'I'm sorry I upset you earlier. I wasn't trying to
imply anything when I remarked on your jewellery. I
knew you'd bought it yourself.'

Catherine eyed him questioningly. 'Then what did
you mean?'

'It's just that when I realised it was genuine, it
struck me what a waste it was when you gave up your
career. Do you realise how many people can only
dream of ever achieving the kind of success you

walked away from? What's that old saying—a broken heart for every light on Broadway? You had everything and you turned your back on it.'

'Money and success aren't everything, Kent.'

'I know they aren't, but you must have wanted them in the beginning or you'd never have got as far as you did.'

'Well, I don't want them any more,' Catherine retorted. 'All I want is to be left alone, allowed to have my shop and run my life the way I want without interference from you.'

'Even when it's for your own good?'

'Oh, you really worry about my "good", don't you? Five minutes ago you were threatening to take away my business!'

Kent sighed impatiently. 'I didn't mean that, Cat. I lost my temper. You were spoiling for a fight from the moment I walked into your apartment. I shouldn't have let you bait me, but . . .' He picked up her hand and gave it a little shake. 'Can't we stop arguing? I'm not going to take your shop away. I'm going to help you with your business.'

Catherine tugged her hand free, her mouth set. 'I wish you'd just leave me alone. I didn't want to come here tonight.'

'You're going to enjoy it, so stop looking like you're going to your execution. If you're acting like this because I'm going to introduce you as Cat Devlin, then stop it. At least give my friends credit for enough sophistication not to act like a bunch of groupies at a rock concert just because you used to be a singer.' When her expressiosn remained unchanged, he suddenly pulled her to him and planted a brief, hard kiss on her lips.

Struggling free, Catherine swore at him. 'Damn

you, you promised you wouldn't touch me!'

Kent laughed lightly, smiling with satisfaction. 'At least I got some colour in your cheeks—now smile,' he coaxed, 'we're here.' The elevator doors opened, and seething with frustrtation, Catherine followed him out. Reaching the door of the penthouse, Kent rang the bell, glancing down at her. 'I said, smile.'

She stared up at him mutinously, but when he stepped towards her, she quickly pasted a smile on her face. The door opened: the ordeal had begun.

CHAPTER FIVE

'YOU can't imagine how pleased I was when I heard you were going to be here tonight.' The woman stepped slightly closer to Catherine, enveloping her in a cloud of rather sickly sweet floral perfume. Automatically, Catherine edged away, only to find herself backed against the black onyx fireplace. She was a great believer in personal space and nothing made her more uncomfortable than having someone intrude on it, especially a stranger.

Her eyes searched the living-room, looking for Kent. When they had arrived earlier, Catherine had been surprised by their host's apartment. A penthouse suite on False Creek, it was furnished in a unique, avant-garde style. The chairs and sofas scattered over the bright yellow carpet seemed more like weird leather and wood sculptures than places to sit. The end tables were fashioned from chrome and glass, their surfaces at present littered with glasses and overflowing ashtrays. Modern abstract paintings, highlighted by discreet hidden lights, provided splashes of colour on the stark white walls.

She finally spotted Kent standing several feet away, deep in conversation with another man. Though she managed to catch his eye, he merely smiled across at her before returning his attention to the other man. No hope of rescue in that quarter, she thought bitterly. He was probably delighted that she was trapped by this old bat.

'These parties are usually so dull,' the woman

standing next to her confided. 'The men always go off in some corner and talk sports or politics, leaving us wives to our own devices.' She was an older woman, long past fifty, her matronly figure swathed in heavy brocade. She laid one beringed hand on Catherine's arm, and Catherine tried not to flinch away. 'I'm so delighted that someone interesting has finally been invited. I always admired you and your brother so much. You were such sweet children, it's just tragic the way your career ended. But then I can understand how you must have felt about continuing after your brother was killed. I was wondering . . .'

'I'm sorry, I don't discuss my career,' Catherine interrupted abruptly. 'Now, if you'll excuse me, please?' The woman looked taken aback as she pushed past her and hurriedly crossed the room to Kent's side.

She reached Kent and he slipped an arm around her waist, glancing down at her. His eyes moved over to the woman she had been talking to, a frown line forming between them as he noticed the woman's flushed, slightly indignant face. He turned back to the man he had been talking to and said, 'Why don't we continue this later? I'm going to take Cat around and make sure she's met everyone.'

He moved away, taking Catherine with him. But instead of joining another group, he drew her into a quiet corner behind a large potted fig tree. 'What did you say to Mrs Gault?' he whispered in an undertone. 'She looks like you insulted her.'

'Well . . . maybe I did. I just . . . I couldn't talk to her any more.' Catherine's hand was shaking as she raised it to brush away a stray lock of hair from her cheek. She felt overwrought and totally unfit to have an argument with Kent right now.

'Look, Cat, I know she can be a tiresome old biddy, but can't you make an effort to get along with her? Her husband is a very important man, and you aren't helping me any by snubbing her.'

Catherine looked at him helplessly. She knew Kent was making an effort to control his impatience with her, but she simply didn't know how to explain that she couldn't cope with the woman's prying questions any longer. Before she could even begin to frame some sort of defence for her action, someone chuckled behind her, 'So this is where you two got to!'

Catherine looked around in relief to find that their host had come over to them. 'Sorry, but you two will have to break it up. Dinner's about to be announced and I'm going to claim my privilege as host to take this lovely lady away from you.'

'Only for dinner, though,' Kent said easily, dropping a light kiss on Catherine's brow before relinquishing her to Peter. His eyes glinted with mockery as Catherine gave him a cutting look before allowing Peter to escort her away. That possessive little gesture had been totally uncalled for!

At dinner, Catherine found herself seated at her host's right hand, and was more than a little amused to find Kent placed at the far end of the table next to Mrs Gault.

She felt a certain satisfaction in knowing that he was the one who would have to cope with the woman's cloying manner and personal remarks throughout the meal. A few minutes later she stole a surreptitious glance in Kent's direction to see how he was getting on. It was rather disappointing to see he seemed to be enjoying himself—although she realised that it had more to do with the blonde seated on his other side than with Mrs Gault.

She turned her attention back to the clear soup she had been eating, suddenly not feeling very hungry. Somehow, in the last weeks she had managed to forget all those orders for flowers. Stealing another peep at the couple, she wondered if that girl had been the recipient of any of them. They made a striking couple, their heads bent close together, one dark, one fair, her hand resting lightly on his arm. Catherine forced another spoonful of soup to her mouth, trying to ignore the lilt of feminine laughter that drifted from the other end of the table. How could she possibly let herself be jealous when for all his talk of friendship, Kent had made it plain that he was more interested in her name than he was in her? Yet she was jealous, painfully so.

'I must say I approve of Kent's taste,' a low voice at her elbow said.

'I'm sorry, what did you say?' Catherine looked up to find her host studying her, a faint smile on his lips. With sudden resolve she smiled back at him, far more warmly than necessary. Two could play at this game, she thought defiantly, refusing to let her eyes travel to the other end of the table where Kent was flirting with the blonde.

'I was just admiring Kent's taste in women,' Peter explained. In spite of herself, Catherine glanced in Kent's direction, her smile fading. At her sudden change of expression, Peter quickly interjected, 'Good lord, you can't think I meant Natalie?'

'She is very attractive,' Catherine replied huskily, wincing inwardly as she saw Kent throw back his head and laugh at some remark the blonde had made.

'But hardly competition,' Peter assured her drily. 'Take my word for it, Kent will ditch her as soon as dinner's over. All he's talked about for the last month

is Cat Devlin. I thought he was never going to stop
keeping you to himself!'

Catherine murmured something unintelligible and
concentrated on her soup. So Kent had talked to Peter
about her. She wondered what he had said. She didn't
have to wait long to find out.

'Kent tells me you'll be helping him with his
campaign,' Peter said, 'so I guess we'll be seeing quite
a bit of one another over the next few months. Did he
mention that I work for him?'

Catherine shook her head. What did he mean, she
would be helping with the campaign? she wondered.
She had only agreed to meet his friends—that was all!

'I'm his campaign manager,' Peter explained, then
added, 'He seems to think you'll be quite an asset.'

Something in the tone of his voice caused her to look
at him. He was smiling at her, yet she sensed he didn't
share Kent's opinion. Well, good! She told herself.
Maybe he would convince Kent to leave her alone.

Curiously enough, though, she felt the stirrings of
anger. Cat Devlin hadn't been some two-bit cabaret
singer. The Devlins had been one of the most popular
acts ever to grace the Las Vegas stage. More often
than not, the show had been sold out weeks in
advance. If she *wanted* to, she could be quite valuable
to Kent's campaign.

The maid brought them another course, and when
she had departed, Catherine remarked on Peter's
unique apartment, deciding she didn't really want to
discuss Kent's career or her possible contribution to it
at this juncture.

Peter looked up from his plate and grinned at her.
'It grows on you after a time. My sister Leanne
decorated it for me, and I'll admit I almost killed her
when I first saw it. I was playing football for the B.C.

Lions at the time and was away for spring training. When I got back, this is what I found.' His arm swept round in an all-encompassing gesture, his expression wry. 'I didn't think I'd ever be able to stand living here, but now that I'm used to it, I kind of like it.' He grinned conspiratorially at her. 'I'd never admit that to Leanne, though!'

The next course was served and it was a few minutes before they resumed their conversation. 'One thing I'll say for my sister,' Peter commented, as Catherine sampled the plate of seafood the maid had placed in front of her, 'she found me a great stereo. I'm a real music nut. You'll have to have Kent bring you around some time to hear my record collection. I even have some of your albums!'

Catherine swallowed the piece of shrimp she had been chewing with some difficulty. Did all conversational roads lead back to Cat Devlin? Finally she managed to say in a bright voice, 'So you're the one. I wondered who had them.'

Peter laughed, then chided her, 'You shouldn't be so modest.'

Her lips twisted into a wry smile. 'Actually, it's not far from the truth. We did well with our stage show, but the albums were a disaster. The expenses that went into producing and promoting them ate up all the profits.'

'Really?' he commented thoughtfully. 'That surprises me. I would have thought your records would have done well.'

Catherine shrugged. 'I guess they didn't sell that badly, but we had one of those deals where just about everyone made money except us.' There was a tinge of bitterness in her tone. Rick had made plenty of money out of the records. She and Casey had given him complete control over their finances and it wasn't until after Casey's death that she had learned just how he had used that control for his own ends. Nothing illegal, of course, Rick was too clever for that; just investments that went sour, expenses that overran. Had it not been for her jewellery, she would have been almost broke when she quit—after five years as one of the highest-paid stars in Las Vegas history.

Peter's attention was claimed by the guest on his other side and when he turned back to her, the subject changed and the rest of the meal passed pleasantly without returning to the topic of Catherine's former career.

Coffee was served in the lounge following dinner, and as soon as she had seated herself on one of the sofas, Kent claimed the space beside her, leaving a disgruntled Natalie to find her own seat. The conversation remained general and Catherine sipped her coffee quietly, not joining in. Though she hated to admit it, she was enjoying herself. She had had to field a few questions about her former career naturally, but except for Mrs Gault's, they hadn't been the prying sort. Actually she felt quite proud of herself. She had answered Kent's friends' questions quite calmly. Perhaps he would realise now that she didn't need to get her past into 'perspective' but simply preferred being Catherine Delaney, florist, to being Cat Devlin, singer.

After coffee the party started to break up and Kent turned and asked her if she were ready to leave. Catherine nodded and when he had helped her to her feet, Kent asked softly, 'It's not been that much of an ordeal, has it?'

Smiling faintly, Catherine shook her head. 'No, I . . . enjoyed it.'

Kent squeezed her hand, grinning at her. 'Good girl! Let's go and say goodbye to Peter.'

Peter was standing near the door making his farewell to the Gaults. He waved them off, then gave his attention to Kent and Catherine. 'You two off now?'

'I think so,' said Kent. 'I've got a big day tomorrow, and I'm sure Cat does too. Everything seemed to go well, don't you think?'

Peter agreed, then said to Catherine, 'I'm glad you came. As I said earlier, I expect we'll be seeing a lot more of each other in the near future. Perhaps we can all get together for lunch one day this week and discuss your part in Kent's campaign. There's a major charity ball coming up next month that——'

'As you said, we'll discuss it over lunch,' Kent interrupted hastily, shifting a quick glance at Catherine. 'Call me tomorrow and we'll arrange a date. Let's go, Cat.' With a firm hand under her elbow, he quickly led Catherine from the apartment.

In the corridor, she jerked away and turned to glare at him. 'What was Peter going to say?' she demanded. 'I agreed to meeting your friends, that was all. Yet all night long Peter has been making remarks about my helping in your campaign. What are you planning?'

'We can't talk here, Cat.' Taking her arm Kent started towards the elevator. 'We can discuss this when we get back to your apartment.'

Catherine would have continued to argue, but another couple came out of Peter's apartment just then, and she realised Kent was right—they couldn't talk here. Once they reached her apartment, though, he wasn't going to put her off.

The drive to her place was completed in frozen silence and as soon as Kent had parked the Mercedes,

SHADOWS IN THE LIMELIGHT

Catherine jumped out and slammed the door behind her. Once Kent joined her on the sidewalk, she turned on her heel and stalked into the building, leaving him to follow. In her apartment, the door closed behind them, she turned on him.

'What was Peter talking about?' she demanded. 'What's this about my helping on your campaign?'

Kent ran an impatient hand around the back of his neck. 'What are you so angry about? We discussed this last night. You agreed to continue seeing me, to appear at my side at social functions.'

'And we need to discuss that over lunch with Peter?' Catherine asked sarcastically. 'You two are cooking up something. What was Peter going to say about that charity do?'

'There's a charity ball in Victoria in a couple of weeks. Since there'll be a lot of reporters there, we just want to discuss the kind of questions they'll be asking you and how you'll answer them. It's no big deal.'

Catherine stared at him, appalled. No big deal! During her career Catherine had maintained an amicable relationship with the press, enjoying the attention afforded her as a popular entertainer. That relationship had changed radically with Casey's death. Shattered by her brother's death and Rick's revelation about his drug problem, she hadn't been able to cope with the prying questions of the press and had taken refuge in anger. They hadn't taken her failure to co-operate lightly, especially when she refused to participate in the mock circus that was supposed to have been her brother's funeral, and had retaliated by crucifying her in the press.

'I'm not going, Kent. You said I'd have to meet your friends, go to a few parties with you. I never agreed to talk to reporters.'

'You're not going to be interviewed,' he said impatiently. 'They'll just want to ask you a couple of questions. You know the sort of thing. Look, the whole idea is to let it be known we're dating and this ball is a good opportunity.'

Catherine had turned away from him and was shaking her head. 'Talking to reporters, letting them pry into my life—that wasn't part of our deal.'

Kent swore suddenly. 'You and that stupid deal!' he lashed out angrily. 'Can't you see things from my point of view for a change? We could get a lot of good publicity out of this. Hell, if you would co-operate, we could even have you sing a couple of songs with the band. That would make a fantastic impression, get your name ...'

'No!' Catherine swung around, screaming the word at him. 'No! I told you I would not appear professionally. I won't!'

'Why not? I heard you in the shop that day, and your voice is as good as ever it was. I'm not suggesting a full-scale show, just one or two songs. It's for charity. With a little rehearsal ...'

'I'm not singing!' Catherine's voice rose to a hysterical pitch. The thought of Rick finding her made her feel trapped. 'And I'm not talking to reporters, either. You can just forget the whole thing.'

'Be reasonable, Cat.' His tone was clipped.

'No!' Catherine cried. She was shaking with the force of her emotions, fear uppermost, as she felt the trap closing on her. Dropping her head, she pressed trembling fingers to her cheeks. In a choked whisper she pleaded, 'I can't, Kent. You can threaten me, take away my store, I don't care. Nothing you can do or say can make me do this.'

Kent stared at her, his anger dissolving. Her face

was completely without colour and her eyes were dark with anguish. Going to her, he rested his hands on her shoulders. 'Shh, calm down,' he coaxed gently.

'I never agreed to sing.' Tears clung to her lashes, then dropped to streak down her cheeks. She looked up at him, her vision blurred by tears. 'You can't make me. I won't go back! I won't be Cat Devlin again. When Casey died, that was the end of it, it was over.' Her voice had sunk to a whisper and Kent pulled her to his chest. A sob shuddered through her and she buried her face in his shoulder.

'Shh,' he whispered gently. He stroked her hair, running his fingers through the silken strands. With it loose, she looked more than ever like the child, Cat Devlin—except for the eyes. There were shadows in them that dimmed the laughter—shadows that would have to remain, secrets untold. He was a fighter, he didn't give up easily, but he knew that for the time being, he had no other choice.

'Don't cry, Cat.' A tremor ran through her and his arms tightened protectively around her. 'Hush now, I won't force you. We'll go back to the way things were before. We'll forget all about business deals and political campaigns. Just don't cry any more.'

Catherine stood on her toes, straining to reach the box at the back of the shelf. The step ladder teetered precariously under her and she grasped the edge of the shelf to retain her balance. The shop's location had a lot of advantages, but storage space wasn't one of them. The store room was hardly bigger than a cupboard and it seemed that whatever Catherine happened to need at any time was generally located at the back of the top shelf. In this case it was a box of ribbons with Happy New Year printed in gay colours across them.

It was three days before Christmas and business had been brisk all morning with poinsettias flowing out of the shop in a red tide that had kept everyone busy. Fortunately, after lunch the stream of customers had diminished, allowing Catherine to gather together the supplies she wanted to take home with her. The florist would be closed for the Christmas-Boxing day holidays, but Catherine planned to make a start on preparing her New Year arrangements during the break. She made another attempt to reach the box, bouncing slightly on the ladder to reach it.

'What in the world are you doing?' A familiar voice demanded from behind her.

Startled, she spun around, her skirt swirling around her knees. Kent was standing in the doorway, his eyes moving over the long length of her legs. Her mouth went dry as she read the look in those eyes, but his expression quickly changed to one of anger as he looked up. 'For God's sake, Cat,' he snapped impatiently, 'are you trying to break your neck?' He crossed the room and put his hands on her waist to lift her off the stepladder.

Catherine wet her lips, her pulse starting to beat a familiar tattoo at his nearness. Seeing him again only brought home how much she had missed him. A few days after Peter's dinner party, Kent had called to explain that he had been unexpectedly called out of town and would see her when he returned. As the days grew into weeks without so much as a postcard from him, Catherine grew convinced the trip was merely an excuse for not seeing her. Once he knew that she wasn't going to let him exploit her as Cat Devlin, he had no further use for her.

Three weeks of silence—her temper flared. What right had he to walk in and out of her life like this? She was just beginning to accept that it was over and now, suddenly, he was back in her life. 'It's my neck. If I want to break it, I will,' she snapped waspishly, automatically trying to twist out of his hold. The action only served to put her off balance. Her hands went to his shoulders to steady herself and he lifted her easily from the stepladder.

He kept her in the circle of his arms, looking down searchingly at her face. She stared at him in confusion. His face was close to hers and now she could see the lines of fatigue that etched its handsome contours. His features suddenly relaxed and he smiled down at her. 'Did you miss me half as much as I missed you, Cat?' he asked softly. Slowly, he drew her to him and lowered his head. His lips were soft and warm as they moved slowly against hers. Gradually the gentle exploration hardened to demand, sending desire flaming through her. Unconsciously she pressed against him, moulding her pliant form to his hard male one. Her arms slipped around him, her fingers kneading the firm muscles of his back. She had missed him, more than she imagined possible. He had become part of her life, a very important part. She needed this contact with him, the reassurance of his heart beating against her, the warmth generated by his touch. She didn't know why he was here, all she knew was that, however much she wished otherwise, she loved him. She needed him.

When he lifted his head his face was slightly flushed. 'I do believe you *have* missed me, Cat,' he said triumphantly.

Hastily Catherine stepped out of his embrace, quite unable to meet his eyes. How could she have let him catch her off guard like that? Obviously that shared moment had meant nothing to him. Embarrassed, she smoothed the folds of her skirt with shaking hands. Clearing her throat, she finally said, 'You're not supposed to kiss me, remember.'

'I forgot.' He grinned at her, giving the lie to the words. 'Are you saying you didn't enjoy your Christmas kiss?' he mocked, and she gave him a withering look. Suddenly, one arm snaked out and wrapped itself around her waist. Pulling her to him, Kent planted a brief, hard kiss on her astonished mouth. When he released her, he laughed down at her, saying, 'Was that better, or shall I try again?'

Quickly Catherine shook her head, edging away from him. 'How did your trip go?' she asked, swiftly changing the subject.

He shrugged noncommittally and once again Catherine saw how tired he looked. 'It was interesting, but I'm glad to be back. I would have called you while I was away, but there never seemed to be an opportunity.'

'Did you get all your business taken care of?'

He sighed rubbing the side of his face in a weary gesture. 'It wasn't a business trip.'

'Oh.' So he had been away on holiday. Catherine didn't know why that should annoy her, but it did. Here she had been, feeling sorry for him because he looked so tired! If he was tired it was probably from too much wine, women and song.

As if reading her thoughts, an amused light entered Kent's eyes. 'Think I've been living it up in some tropical paradise?' he teased. 'I haven't, I went to China.'

'Where?'

'China.' He grinned as she eyed him with disbelief.

'I've been touring China with a group of businessmen for the last two weeks. I didn't mention it before because I had originally decided not to go. I didn't think I could fit it into my schedule, but I changed my mind. There was still a space available on the tour, so I went.'

He averted his eyes momentarily, wondering what her reaction would be if he told her what had changed his mind. Their last evening together, when she had cried in his arms, had been a turning point for him. She had awakened something in him he hadn't thought he possessed. For the first time in his life he felt protective towards a woman. The trip had been a last-ditch attempt to convince himself that he could forget her, that his feelings were momentary. But even with the Pacific Ocean between them and the wonders of an ancient culture to distract him, she had filled his thoughts. When he looked back he saw the face that had haunted him all the time he had been away.

Moving to her, he lowered his head to brush her lips with his, then said, 'I missed you, Cat, and now I've got to go away again. I stopped in to let you know I have to leave for my parents' house in Victoria this afternoon. I'm spending the holidays with them, so I brought you your Christmas present today. I left it out front.'

Catherine lowered her lashes so that he couldn't read her reaction to his going away again in her eyes. Training her lips into an unconcerned smile, she stepped away from him and in a determinedly cheerful voice said, 'I'm afraid your gift isn't here. I left it at my apartment.' She didn't know why she had even found him something, because she had been sure he had dropped out of her life. Nonetheless, she had taken a pair of cufflinks that had been Casey's from her safety

deposit box and wrapped them to give to him just in
case. They were made of gold and set with sapphires,
and she wasn't sure why she wanted him to have them.
She had never given any of Casey's jewellery away and
even when she had sold some of her own pieces to raise
enough capital to start her florist's, she had kept all of
her brother's jewellery.

'Don't worry about it. You can give it to me when I
get back.'

'Of course.' Catherine turned away from him, idly
rearranging the florist supplies she had placed in a
carton.

'What was it you wanted from the shelf when I
came in?' he asked, coming up behind her. 'I'll get it
down for you before I leave.'

'That's OK,' she declined. 'Jerry, my delivery boy,
will help me.' She felt curiously flat and had an
overwhelming desire to be alone.

'I don't mind,' Kent insisted, stepping on to the
stepladder. 'Just tell me what you want.'

It seemed futile to argue, so she said, 'That blue box
at the back.'

He reached it easily and handed it to her, watching
while she placed it in the carton with her other
supplies. 'You're taking those home with you?' he
asked.

'Yes.' She nodded. 'I've got a lot of orders for New
Year parties and I'm going to get started on them over
the break.'

His eyes narrowed. 'I assumed you would be going
away for the holidays.'

'Well . . .' Catherine said awkwardly. Months ago,
she and Nancy had tentatively planned to go skiing
over the break, but that idea had ended with their
friendship. On the other hand, she didn't want Kent to

know that she was at a loose end, so she finally prevaricated. 'There isn't really time to go away. I'm only closing for three days.'

'Where are you spending Christmas Day?'

Catherine hesitated, not quite knowing what to say.

'Cat, you haven't any plans,' Kent stated suddenly, obviously reading her hesitation correctly. 'Since that's the case, you can come to Victoria.' The thought of spending the holidays with her made his blood sing.

'Come to Victoria?' Catherine echoed.

'I think you would enjoy it.'

'Oh.' Now he was feeling sorry for her. She frowned at the idea. 'Well, thank you for the invitation, but I don't think so.'

'Why not? You haven't any other plans, have you?'

'Actually, I have.' She didn't look at him. She was telling the truth, wasn't she? 'I have a lot of work to catch up on over the holidays.'

'Don't be ridiculous, Catherine. Even Scrooge took Christmas Day off,' he said impatiently.

'Oh, Kent!' She turned to look at him, disgusted with herself for finding the invitation appealing. She didn't want his pity. But she couldn't bring herself to refuse his invitation straight out, and finally hedged, 'Maybe if you had asked me earlier I would have considered it, but not at such short notice. I can't just land on your family for Christmas. I'm an outsider, I wouldn't be comfortable.'

'Please, Cat. It's time you met my family,' he argued.

'I don't think so,' she protested, though she felt her resolve weakening. 'I haven't anything to take for them and it's too late to go Christmas shopping now.'

'They won't expect you to come laden with presents, Cat. They'll understand that you haven't had any notice.' He smiled at her, coaxing. 'Please, Cat. If you don't come, it will spoil my Christmas.'

'Don't be silly,' Catherine snapped. 'Why should you care how I choose to spend the holiday?'

He reached up and touched the faint blue smudge under her eye, frowning suddenly. 'I'll worry about you if I know you're here on your own,' he admitted softly. 'You look tired, Cat. You should have more help in the shop. I bet you haven't taken a day off for weeks.'

She wrenched away from his touch, putting her back to him. Damn him, she didn't need his pity. 'Look, you don't have to feel sorry for me,' she said in a strained voice. 'I never have put much emphasis on Christmas. I want to spend the day in my own fashion.'

'I'm not leaving you here alone,' he said stubbornly, his mouth set with determination. 'I know you, your idea of spending the day in your own fashion would be to keep on working.'

'Don't try to bully me, Kent. It's nothing to you what I do. Can't you just leave me alone?'

'No, Cat, I can't,' he shot back, suddenly losing his temper. 'Now, you're coming with me to Victoria whether you want to or not.'

'I am not!' she retorted, glaring at him.

His eyes clashed with hers, then suddenly his softened. 'Did you know your eyes shoot out little gold sparks when you're angry?' He laughed, his expression suddenly indulgent. 'That was one of the first things I noticed about you.' Ignoring her defiant stance, he gently pulled her into his arms and held her firmly when she would have struggled free. His eyes warmed to a soft blue as he held her gaze. 'It's almost Christmas, let's not fight any more. Can't we call a truce for a few days?' He kissed her lightly, holding her closely to him. 'Please, Cat, let's be friends,' he whispered against her hair.

She felt herself weaken. It would be a lonely Christmas if she refused to go with him. And she really did want to spend the time with him. 'OK, Kent, I'll come with you,' she gave in grudgingly.

CHAPTER SIX

SEVERAL hours later, Catherine was leafing through a magazine while Kent read the evening papers. She wasn't quite sure how he had managed to override all her objections, so that now she found herself on the B.C. ferry heading out of Tsawwassen. She had agreed to spend Christmas Day with him, yet somehow he had manoeuvred her into spending several days with him and his parents. Paula had been left in charge of the shop and would prepare any last-minute orders, Jerry would serve in the front of the shop, and Paula's husband, who had been laid off from his regular job, had been pressed into service as the delivery man. So much for considering herself indispensable!

It was after nine that evening when they reached his parents' house just outside Victoria. The senior Latimers' home was located on the water in an exclusive area of the Saanich Peninsula. Kent had described the house to her before they had left Vancouver, explaining that his parents had had it custom-built for them only a few years ago. However, when he pulled the car into the drive, it was not the ultra-modern cedar and glass edifice that caught her attention, but the numerous cars parked in front of it.

She felt her spirits wavering as she turned to look at Kent in the silence after he had switched off the motor. He seemed totally unsurprised to find the driveway lined with cars, the house blazing with lights. 'Are your parents entertaining?' she asked quietly, telling herself that she shouldn't jump to conclusions.

'I thought I mentioned that they would probably have a houseful. They do a lot of entertaining around Christmas,' he returned matter-of-factly, removing the keys from the ignition and getting out of the car. As he walked round the car to help her out, Catherine felt a sense of bitterness and deep disappointment wash over her. She should have realised that Kent's invitation was far from altruistic. He couldn't care less how she spent her Christmas: he had only asked her to accompany him so he would have an opportunity to display Cat Devlin.

Kent opened the passenger door and reached out to help her from the car. Although she had attempted to school her expression, he frowned when he saw her face in the car light. 'Is something wrong, Cat?' he asked as she stepped from the car, ignoring his extended hand.

'Of course not,' Catherine snapped, 'although didn't you say even Scrooge took Christmas off?'

He muttered something under his breath. 'Being around you is like working in a dynamite factory! I never know what's going to set you off. Would you mind explaining what that remark was supposed to mean?' He gripped her arm, forcing her to remain with him.

'You could at least have been honest.' Her voice wavered as she tried to pull away from him. 'If you wanted me to be Cat Devlin for you, you should have said so, instead of feeding me all that nonsense about not wanting me to spend Christmas alone.'

'It wasn't nonsense, Cat,' Kent insisted, holding her firmly in an embrace. 'I was worried about you. You don't take care of yourself like you should. I thought

bringing you with me—the break—would do you good
. . . get rid of some of those shadows under your eyes.
I had no idea that you'd be upset just because my
parents are having a party.' She turned her head, not
wanting him to see the tears of hurt that had filmed
her eyes. 'Cat, you don't have to go to the party. We'll
just say hello to my parents and then you can go to your
room. I'm not expecting anything from you other than
that you relax and enjoy yourself over the next few
days.'

Catherine remained silent, wanting desperatcly to
believe him. She didn't resist as he pulled her gently
against his chest, his hand stroking her back in a
soothing gesture. 'Don't be upset, honey,' he said
softly. 'I want you to have a happy Christmas.'
Comforted by the arms around her, she gradually
relaxed. Feeling the tension drain out of her, Kent
held her slightly away from him and looked down at
her. 'Feel better?'

She nodded, managing a faint smile. He returned it,
then dropped a gentle kiss on her forehead. 'Let's go
inside.' With his arm still firmly around her waist he
led her towards the front door. As they mounted the
steps it was flung open and a small, silver-haired
woman came out to greet them.

'So you finally got here! We thought you would take
an earlier ferry.' Although she had addressed Kent,
her eyes were studying Catherine with undisguised
curiosity. Catherine flushed slightly under her scru-
tiny, thankful she had taken the time to renew her
make-up and comb her hair before they had left the
ferry. Her beige trouser suit was still relatively fresh,
though she was uncomfortably aware that it was
painfully casual compared with the elegant hostess
gown the other woman wore. Nonetheless, the woman

smiled at her approviongly and said, 'You must be Cat Devlin. I'm Kent's mother, Jean Latimer, but please, call me Jean—then I can call you Cat.' She held out her hand and shook Catherine's hand enthusiastically, then drew them inside with her.

'Ever since Kent called to say he was bringing you with him I've been dying to meet you,' she said, helping Catherine remove her coat. 'I've heard so much about you.' She spoke rapidly, raising her voice slightly to be heard over the party noises drifting into the hall from the rear of the house. 'Kent, you bring in the luggage, while I take Cat in to introduce her to our guests. They've been just as anxious to meet her as I have.'

Catherine shot Kent a pleading look as his mother started away still chattering like a chipmunk. 'Mother!' Kent interrupted her in a stern voice, and Mrs Latimer swung around to face her son. 'We're not going to the party.'

'What do you mean? Certainly you'll come to the party. Everyone is expecting you.' Her expression was plainly dismayed as she looked from Kent to Catherine.

'Kent?' Catherine said uncertainly.

He came over to her and put his arm possessively around her waist. 'Mother, Cat's tired. I'm going to take her to her room. Where have you put her?'

At the firmness of his tone, Mrs Latimer looked deflated, making Catherine feel even worse than if she had continued to argue. Though there was little resemblance between mother and son, they shared the same startling blue eyes and the expression in Mrs Latimer's was now clearly disappointed.

After a moment, however, she smiled warmly at Catherine. 'Forgive me, Cat. Of course you're tired.

I've put you in the room next to Kent's and can show it to you while Kent brings in your cases.'

The bedroom Mrs Latimer took her to was on the second floor, overlooking the water. It was comfortable and spacious, decorated in an attractive shade of pale blue with darker blue accents. White French provincial furniture and Austrian brocade curtains gave a pleasantly feminine note to the room.

While pointing out the bathroom down the hall and showing Catherine where she could find extra blankets if she needed them, Mrs Latimer couldn't have been friendlier—or made Catherine feel guiltier. Jean Latimer was genuinely disappointed that she wasn't going to be able to introduce Catherine to her friends. More to the point, though, Catherine had the distinct impression it was *not* Cat Devlin she wanted to introduce, but her son's friend she wanted her guests to meet. Jean Latimer was clearly a devoted mother and Catherine felt she would have probably welcomed Lucrezia Borgia with open arms, if she thought Kent was friends with the woman.

When Mrs Latimer had assured herself that Catherine was comfortably settled and was preparing to leave, Catherine's conscience finally got the better of her. Smiling at her hostess, she agreed to put in an appearance at the party after she had had a chance to change into something more suitable. Delighted, the older woman left her to return to her guests.

Kent arrived with her suitcases a few minutes later and Catherine quickly opened the door in response to his knock, mentally reviewing the clothes she had brought with her. If Mrs Latimer's gown had been any indication, she would definitely be out of place if she went downstairs in the trouser suit she was wearing.

Perhaps one of the evening dresses she had brought
with her would have survived the indignity of being
folded into a suitcase without becoming too wrinkled.

Kent deposited her cases on the chest at the end of
the bed. 'I'm sorry about my mother, Cat. I guess I
should have warned you.' He came to stand behind
her, his hands coming up to massage the muscles of
her neck. 'Don't worry about her, I'll go down and
have a talk with her. You go ahead and get ready for
bed.'

His fingers were soothing as he kneaded the tension
from her shoulders, sending a gentle wave of languor
flowing through her. She knew she should tell him that
she had already agreed to attend his mother's party,
but for a moment she only wanted to bask in his gentle
concern. Kent could be so *nice* when he wanted to,
thought Catherine, resisting the urge to lean back
against him.

As her blood quickened under the fingers caressing
the back of her neck, she wondered how she could
have been so foolish as to think she could keep their
relationship on a platonic level. Reacting against her
mother's lifestyle, Catherine had developed a decidedly old-fashioned attitude towards the physical
relationship between men and women. Until she met
Kent, she had never imagined that she would be
tempted to ignore her scruples under the influence of
desire. She hadn't realised the powerful need a man
could awaken in a woman who loved him.

When Kent pushed aside the fall of hair that
covered her nape and his lips brushed against the
sensitive flesh he had exposed, a frisson of pleasure
rippled down her spine. His arms slipped around her,
pulling her back against him until she could feel the
hard muscles of his thighs. His mouth journeyed along

the tender curve of her neck and his hands moved upward to stroke her breasts gently through her silk shirt.

A shudder passed through her as desire rippled along her nerve ends and her breathing became harsh and uneven. Kent slipped his hand inside her blouse, delighting her as he touched her soft flesh; helpless to control her reaction, she relaxed against him. His fingers were cool against her heated skin as he stroked the nipple erect, kneading the fullness with his palms.

With a soft groan, he slowly turned her to face him, moulding her yielding curves to his firm ones, and finding her mouth with his. There was an urgency to his kiss as he parted her lips, dragging a primitive response from the very depths of her. 'Oh, Cat,' he whispered against her lips. 'Do you have any idea what you do to me?'

As he kissed her his fingers found the buttons of her blouse and deftly unfastened them. Pushing it aside, he lowered his head to her exposed breast and took it in his mouth, his tongue tracing an exquisite circle that sent painful pleasure shooting through her. Her pulse was pounding in her ears as she strained against him, lost in a rapture of pure sensation. He slipped the top from her shoulders, letting it fall to the floor, and buried his face in the scented flesh between her breasts. His jaw was faintly rough from the day's growth of beard, awakening her senses with exquisite delight.

Easily, he lifted her off her feet and laid her across the satin spread on the bed. For a long moment he held her eyes, then moved them slowly over her bare flesh in a look akin to a caress. 'You're so very beautiful, Cat,' he said softly. 'I don't think I could ever tire of looking at you.' In a fluid movement he lay on the bed beside her, stroking the satin flesh of her midriff as his eyes roved over the rounded curve of her breasts. Catherine stared at him in mute appeal, the depth of her need almost painful. Her breasts felt full and heavy as his gaze touched them, and she ached for his touch. She raised her hands and linked them around his neck, her lips parting invitingly. The kiss was long and drugged, filled with the heat of passion that burned between them.

Her blood was drumming in her ears, shutting out reality, when Kent suddenly jack-knifed off the bed, muttering a curse. Someone was knocking at the door, then: 'Cat, are you about ready to come down?' Mrs Latimer's voice was strident as it came through the closed door of the bedroom.

For several seconds, Catherine stared at the door-knob in horror. She didn't dare breathe for fear it would turn and Mrs Latimer would come in uninvited. Kent's mind was obviously running on parallel lines, because he suddenly hissed, 'For God's sake, answer her before she decides to come in!'

His words snapped her trance, and she said quickly, 'D-don't come in, I'm ... I'm just changing. I'll be down in a couple of minutes.' Her voice sounded high-pitched and unnatural.

'OK, then,' Mrs Latimer answered through the door. 'You don't know where Kent is, do you?'

Casting a quick glance at the man standing beside the bed, Catherine quickly lied, 'No-no. I haven't seen him.'

'I'll see if I can find him while you finish dressing,' said Jean. Then they heard her walk away. Turning to look at Kent, Catherine suddenly became aware of the expression in his eyes and blushed crimson as she realised how close they had been to complete love-making. Self-consciously, she gathered the spread around her, too embarrassed to meet his eyes.

His eyes lingered momentarily on her. 'I'd better get out of here,' he said in a strained voice, and turning away abruptly, left the room.

Fifteen minutes later, Catherine was dressed and walking down the corridor to the stairs. She hadn't dressed so fast since her days as a singer when she had had to make quick costume changes between acts. She was wearing a black cocktail dress with a dropped waistline that gave it a faintly 1920s look. The low-cut bodice was held up by narrow shoulder straps and edged with silver sequins. With dark tights and matching shoes, it was very attractive, and Catherine hoped no one would would notice it was slightly creased from lying in her suitcase.

Mrs Latimer was in the hall when she descended the stairs. Immediately, the other woman crossed to her, giving the dress a look of approval. Her faced wreathed with smiles, she looped her arm through Catherine's and impelled her towards the rear of the house. Catherine was faintly bemused by the time they reached the enormous living-room that faced the sea. She would have been disappointed if Kent's mother hadn't liked her, although her wholehearted approval was nearly as disconcerting.

Finally the introductions were completed, and Jean left her with the last group she had met while she went to fetch her a glass of egg-nog. As Catherine listened idly to the small talk flowing around her, she casually inspected the room. It was ideal for entertaining and though there were easily thirty people in the room, it was far from crowded. Huge windows formed one wall, overlooking the water, and Catherine imagined the view of the Gulf Islands would be spectacular in the daylight. Holly boughs decorated the mantel of the stone fireplace where a cheerful fire crackled behind a glass screen. At the opposite end of the room from the fireplace was a magnificent grand piano in gleaming mahogany. Next to it was the Christmas tree, its pine boughs decorated with gold ornaments and lights that colour co-ordinated with the room's furnishings.

The tree almost reached the high, vaulted ceiling and Catherine was speculating as to how they had managed to get it through the door, when she noticed that the group around her had fallen silent. She looked up to meet cold, black eyes staring at her from a mature, handsome face. The family resemblance to Kent was unmistakable and she knew instantly that this man was his father. However, there was none of the friendly acceptance displayed by Mrs Latimer in his face. His expression was faintly censorious, his gaze derogatory as he moved his eyes down her body in insolent appraisal.

'So, you're the famous Cat Devlin,' Mr Latimer said, his eyes returning to her face. Catherine frowned at the cold inflexion of his tone. She looked around to find that the group she had been standing with had quietly faded away. Mrs Latimer was deep in conversation at the far side of the room, her mission of providing Catherine with a drink obviously forgotten. Kent had yet to arrive and Catherine realised she was on her own to deal with the unfriendly man before her.

Catherine licked her lips nervously. 'That was my stage name,' she said finally. 'My real name is Catherine Delaney.' Her chin lifted slightly, her eyes finding his.

'The name Cat Devlin is the one everyone is supposed to have heard, though,' he said smoothly. He paused a moment, his eyes boring into hers and Catherine found she was forced to drop her own. 'My son tells me that you are a great political asset and can make all the difference to his career.'

'He has asked me to help him on his camnpaign,' Catherine said evenly. She didn't want to admit that Kent had later changed his mind. She couldn't understand why James Latimer should have taken such an instant dislike to her, but whatever the cause, the feeling was mutual. His obvious scepticism about her worth as a political supporter rankled.

'In exactly what form is this "help" supposed to come?'

Catherine cleared her throat. 'Accompanying him to various functions, being seen at his side . . .' she hesitated a fraction of a second, then looked squarely into his face, 'letting the public know that I'm the lady in his life.' It was a foolish boast, designed merely to annoy James Latimer, but as she saw his jawline harden she knew it had succeeded and she was secretly pleased with herself for having made it.

His eyes fell to the low neck of her dress, then moved lower to skim the rounded curves of her hips in a purely sexual appraisal. He looked up again, smiling faintly when he saw Catherine's heated cheeks. 'Yes,' he said silkily, 'I have little doubt that there are certain areas of my son's life where he finds you quite useful.'

Catherine drew her breath in sharply. 'I don't think I care for your implication, Mr Latimer.' She saw Kent enter the living-room with Peter Castle and automatically started towards him, wanting only to escape.

As she moved, Mr Latimer's hand shot out to take her wrist in a painful grip. 'Before you go, just one thing, Miss Devlin,' he said in a soft, menacing voice.

'For all your avowals of helping Kent politically, being publicised as the "lady in his life", you have yet to appear at a public function with him.' The hand on her wrist tightened. 'I don't like Kent bringing his little diversions into my home under the guise of a business associate. It's an insult to myself and to my wife. And just because he brought you here, don't be tempted to think it means anything. No has-been entertainer has anything to offer my son on a permanent basis.' His dark eyes glittered like obsidian as he held hers. Abruptly he released her and walked away without a backward glance.

Momentarily stunned, Catherine watched James Latimer join a group standing near the tree. He shot her a look, his eyes contemptuous. As his mouth curled into a faintly satisfied smile, something inside her hardened. James Latimer was clearly telling her that she was not good enough for his son. More than anything else, his taunt that she was a has-been as though she had 'never been' rankled most of all. Her chin rose fractionally as she met James Latimer's stare. She had thought her self-respect, her pride in being Cat Devlin had been destroyed. Finding out about Casey's addiction had destroyed the illusion of perfection that had surrounded the Devlins, an illusion, she realised now, that she had believed in. Had *had* to believe in, to give her the pride necessary to perform. But with Casey's death, and the reason for it, her life had been shown up for what it was—an illusion built on lies. She had hidden her identity, shunned the questions as much from shame as desire to avoid painful memories.

But Kent's father had just shown her that all pride was not dead. Maybe she didn't have the blue blood of the Latimers of this world flowing in her veins, and maybe her brother had been on drugs, but Cat Devlin wasn't a piece of dirt under James Latimer's feet either!

When Kent came over to her, bearing the drink his mother had forgotten, Catherine gave him a warm smile and slipped her arm though his. James Latimer had released something inside. She was Cat Devlin and she wasn't going to pretend otherwise. She had been a good singer and excellent performer. There was pride in that, whatever had happened later. Laughing up at Kent, she gave herself up to the enjoyment of the party.

In the hours that followed, she knew Kent often looked at her with puzzled eyes, unable to fathom the change that had taken place. She laughed frequently, her eyes sparkling, and when someone asked her about her singing career, she didn't retreat behind a wall of silence as she normally did, but answered their queries in an easy, relaxed manner.

When the guests gathered around the piano to sing Christmas carols, Catherine joined them, Kent at her side. It was inevitable that one of the guests request that she do a solo number. For a brief instant, a refusal hovered on her tongue, then she saw James Latimer watching her, his look clearly indicating he expected her to decline. Turning to the pianist, she nodded her head and asked him to play an old classic that would clearly demonstrate the full range of her voice.

The Latimers' living-room bore little resemblance to the main room of a Las Vegas hotel and the accompaniment of a piano played by a social player was totally unlike the backing of a full orchestra. Yet as Catherine neared the end of the first verse, the magic of singing for an audience began to take over. The dozen guests grouped around the piano were no different from the hundreds she had performed for in her life and, in a backswitch of time, Catherine experienced once again that intimate communication between a performer and her audience. Her voice swelled on the high notes of the chorus as she poured her soul into pleasing her listeners. As a performer, a professional, she had an obligation to entertain and as she drew on the resources of her talent, she could feel the surge of warmth that emanates from a captivated audience.

Deep silence greeted the dying of the last note. Then, as the guests recovered and started to applaud, Kent took her hands in his and pulled her to him.

'That was beautiful, Cat,' he said, his voice filled with emotion. His mouth came down on hers in a brief tender kiss before he released her. Automatically Catherine's eyes went to his father's, the triumphant light in them making their own challenge.

Later, seated on the sofa next to Kent while he chatted with Peter Castle, she gave in to her exhaustion. The spurt of bravado that had carried her through the evening had faded, leaving in its wake a profound weariness. Kent was right about one thing: she was tired. Most retail businesses experienced a marked increase in trade in the month before Christmas and hers had been no exception. Yet though she had spent long hours at the store over the last few weeks, she wished suddenly that she was back among the flowers again. She found contentment, peace even, as Catherine Delaney. That was something she never had or would have as Cat Devlin. Cat Devlin lived in a mountainous terrain of emotions. She scaled steep peaks in front of an audience, reaching the summit in that brief moment before the applause broke out. Then the show was over and once again she was plunged back into the valleys. Catherine Delaney's life was lived on a plain of rolling contours. There were no great highs, but neither were there any deep lows.

'Tired?' Kent asked softly, taking her hand in his and giving it a gentle squeeze.

'A little,' Catherine admitted, giving him her attention.

'The party will be breaking up soon. I don't think anyone would object if you went up to your room now.'

She sat up straighter, smoothing her skirt over her knees. 'I think I will, if you don't mind.'

'I'll walk up with you.' Kent stood up and pulled her to her feet and Peter rose with them.

'Before you go,' said Peter, 'I just wanted to say how much I enjoyed your song. You haven't lost your touch over the years.'

Catherine gave him a slight smile. 'Thank you.' She wanted to forget about being Cat Devlin for a while. Maybe I'm one of those split personalities, she thought. Tonight was the first time she had felt like Cat Devlin in years, but now she was feeling like Catherine again. And Catherine wanted to go to her room and not think about Cat.

'No, I think I must thank you,' Peter said graciously. 'The world lost something special when you ended your career. Was it only because you lost your brother?'

Catherine hesitated, checking the impulse to nod her head. She had talked about her career tonight, about Cat Devlin and her life as a singer. Initially she had been uncomfortable, the years of dodging questions, serving up partial truths not easily forgotten. But, at the same time, there had been a certain freedom in speaking openly about the past. Finally she shook her head in answer to Peter's question. 'That was part of it, but there were other factors that made it difficult to continue.'

'What were they?' Kent joined the conversation.

'Oh, a number of things,' Catherine answered, noncommittally. Both men were still watching her with interest, obviously waiting for her to elaborate, so she continued: 'For one thing, I had a falling out with with our manager and didn't want him handling my career any more. I would have had to find a way out of my contract with him and then there was the problem of finding a new manager, so ... it just didn't seem worth it.' She shrugged, then said to Kent, 'I really would like to go to my room now.'

'Of course,' he agreed instantly, taking her arm and escorting her away. On the way out, they stopped near the piano to say goodnight to Mr and Mrs Latimer. Catherine focused her attention on Jean Latimer, accepting her thanks for singing for her guests but all the time aware of the censure in her husband's eyes.

Finally, reluctantly, she turned her attention to Kent's father. Holding out her hand to shake his, she met his eyes bravely. 'Thank you, Mr Latimer, for having me. Goodnight.'

Ignoring her proffered hand, James Latimer said coldly, 'You are my son's guest, Miss Devlin. There's no need to thank me.' Turning on his heel, he stalked to the far side of the room. The three remaining endured an awkward silence for several seconds. Mrs Latimer looked acutely embarrassed, her hands fluttering nervously.

Catherine saw a dull red flush creep up Kent's face as he looked at his father and the muscles of his jaw stood out in hard cords. Over the last weeks she had felt the lash of Kent's temper a number of times and knew he was close to losing it now. He made a slight movement in the direction of his father and Catherine quickly grasped his arm. 'I really do want to go up now . . . please, Kent.' He looked down at her, his eyes still glinting with anger. 'Please,' Catherine repeated, and at last he nodded and led her from the room.

CHAPTER SEVEN

CATHERINE walked slowly up the stairs with Kent at her side. At each step she felt a little stab of guilt. She had known what Kent's father's opinion of her was and she had been deliberately provoking him tonight. Instead of fading into the woodwork, she had consciously drawn attention to herself, to Cat Devlin, all because she had let herself be piqued by James Latimer's opinion of her as a singer.

Casting a surreptitious glance at Kent, she could tell by the set of his mouth that he was still upset. She could feel the tension in him, the anger. Though she occasionally resented him, she didn't want to become a bone of contention between Kent and his father. For five years she had avoided the role of Cat Devlin and when she finally came out of the shadows, it was to make a complete mess of things.

At the door to her room, Kent turned to her, gently resting his hand on her arm when she would have slipped past him and gone inside. For a moment he merely looked down into her upturned face, then said, 'I owe you an apology. I'm sorry about what happened just now.'

Catherine moved her head in a helpless gesture. 'It wasn't your fault.'

He grimaced, running an impatient hand through his dark hair. 'I don't know what got into him, but he shouldn't have talked to you like that. He . . . I want you to understand something, Cat,' he said seriously. 'I'm not going to let it affect my relationship with you, and I don't want you to either. As for my father, I'll make sure he knows he can't be rude to you without answering to me. It won't happen again, OK?'

Catherine stared at his shirt front for a moment, biting her lip for a moment. She was beginning to discover that being in love with someone wasn't always easy. She didn't like James Latimer, hated his blatant snobbery and inherent arrogance. But she loved Kent and knew she couldn't come between him and his father, even if it meant letting James Latimer have what he wanted. 'Maybe it would be better if we just forgot the whole thing,' she said at last.

'What do you mean?'

'I mean . . .' she hesitated, taking a deep breath, 'I mean, your father doesn't like me. It might be better if I just went home, took the ferry back to Vancouver in the morning.'

He shook his head. 'No, Cat. I'm not going to let you run away. My father doesn't run my life. There's been a lot of tension between us over the last few years because he won't accept that. I don't want you to feel that you're creating dissension where none existed before. I invited you here, I'm not going to let him drive you away.'

Catherine hesitated, torn. Perhaps what Kent said was true. That his relationship with his father was strained long before her advent into his life—but there was no getting around the fact that she was the cause of the current animosity between them. She didn't really want to go home, yet she didnt want to be the central figure in a dispute between the Latimers either. Going over what James had said to her earlier, she suddenly asked, 'Do you really think I could help your career, Kent? Be a political asset?'

She saw surprise flicker in Kent's blue eyes, then he

smiled. 'Without doubt, Cat. Tonight your singing, the way you got along with the guests, was fabulous. I was very proud of you. You can help me in a way no one else can. It's not just that you're a beautiful woman and you're talented. You have an image, a reputation that is untarnished. People admire you because you're Cat Devlin, and that admiration rubs off on me when they know I'm the man in your life.'

He hesitated, then continued: 'I've always been interested in government, in politics. When I first started out I thought to be a good politician all you needed were sound ideas and the energy and ambition to see them put into practice. But it doesn't work that way.' His voice dropped to a low intense pitch. 'There are responsible voters, those who know the issues and cast their vote for the man they agree with. But there are an awful lot of people out there who vote on a man's looks, or his speech-making abilities, or maybe just because he has the support of someone they admire . . . like Cat Devlin.' He paused for an instant to let his words sink in. When he continued, his voice was rich with sincerity. He held her eyes, his own fired with the depth of his ambition. 'I still have good ideas, Cat. There's so much I would like to see done in this country. I would like to work for Canada, not as a Westerner or an anglophile but as a Canadian. I think I have a lot to offer, but I have to get elected before I can do anything—and that means votes. You can help me get those.'

Catherine bit her lip. 'I don't know,' she said helplesly. She wanted to help Kent, she realised. Her original agreement to help had come simply because she knew if she didn't, he would stop seeing her. There was more to it now. She knew she was influenced by his father's opinion of her, the near-challenge he had thrown down to her. Partly, it was just loving him and wanting to be with him. But more than that, she believed in him, in his ideas, in his ability to contribute, and she wanted to be a part of it. But if Rick found her . . .

'Don't worry about my father, Cat,' Kent interrupted. 'I can handle him. Your being here for a few days will help. I'm sure once he gets to know you a little better, realises how important you are to me, he'll change his attitude.'

Still she hesitated.

'Listen, Cat, don't make a decision right now, OK? I'll have a talk with my dad. Peter's staying here and we were planning to discuss a game plan for the next few months over the holiday. There's a seat open and we're expecting the Prime Minister to call the by-election for the late spring. My father is going to be joining our sessions. I'd like you to be there too. It will show you both just what Cat Devlin can do for my campaign.' He stepped nearer to her, placing his hands on her shoulders and peering down into her face.

She looked up at him, doubt on her face. She *could* do a lot for his campaign. But she could also ruin it. If the press ever found out about the real reason for Casey's death, or if someone discovered her 'untarnished image' was a lie, it would do Kent irreparable damage. She should tell him now, before it was too late. And have him walk out o her life. She couldn't face that—not now he had come back.

'Give it a try, Cat. Please!'

Slowly, Catherine nodded. After all, if no one had uncovered the truth in Las Vegas, where reputations were shredded every day, it wasn't likely to happen now.

Kent squeezed her shoulder encouragingly, smiling down at her. 'Good girl!' He dropped a quick kiss on her forehead, then said, 'I should get back downstairs. You get some sleep. Goodnight, Cat.' His hands dropped from her and he walked away.

Tucking the magazine she had just purchased from the news-stand under her arm, Catherine went to rejoin Kent and Peter. As she approached their seats, she saw that the two men were deep in conversation. On impulse, she changed direction and slipped through one of the heavy doors out on to the deck of the ferry.

A sharp wind whipped at her hair and she pulled her coat more closely around her throat. The deck was deserted and she moved to find a place protected from the wind. Given that it was only two days past Christmas, the weather was fine despite the bite in the air. The sky over the Gulf Islands was clear blue with only a few high clouds scudding before the breeze.

Catherine leaned against a pillar, her eyes on the islands they passed as the big white car-ferry threaded its way through them on the journey back to Vancouver. It had been an eventful holiday, yet she found she didn't want to think of the recent past now, or the future for that matter—a future tied to the past. A future where she would be Cat Devlin again. She had committed herself to doing all she could for Kent. During long hours spent in his father's study, she had been caught up in Kent's enthusiasm, ensnared by his dreams. If only she would be able to go through with it.

Her thoughts drifted to Casey as she suppressed her uncertainties about being Cat Devlin again, She had thought of him often in these last few days. In odd moments glimpses of him would come to mind: his face; the sound of his laughter the expression in his eyes when he would tease her into losing her temper, then stand back and watch the sparks fly.

She had not really thought about him since his death, had tried to block his image from her mind, but lately she had found herself pondering those last months of his life. Had they really grown so far apart? They had no longer lived together, each having their own apartment, their own friends, but had they truly been estranged? They had seen each other daily, at rehearsals, on stage. Frequently, they had shared meals and outings.

Catherine had known Casey had something on his mind, had sensed his preoccupation. But had it been drugs? She chewed her lip. Her grief, the overwhelming hurt she had experienced at what she felt was Casey's betrayal of her, had shut a door in her mind on her brother's memory. She hadn't let herself think about him. But recently, with the past thrust upon her again . . .

Unconsciously, Catherine shook her head. One could not dispute the evidence. He must have been on drugs, for how else could he have overdosed? As always, her thoughts had led her along the same path, to the same journey's end.

She saw Kent walking along the deck towards her and looked at him with a sense of relief, storing away her memories again. How handsome he was! The wind was ruffling his dark hair and had heightened the colour in his tanned face, giving him a piratical look. He wore a heavy topcoat that did nothing to detract from his lean, muscular build, its dark fur collar turned up to frame his well-formed features. He drew closer and his bright blue eyes lit up as he spied her standing behind the pillar and he quickly came over to her.

'It's freezing out here! What are you doing?'

Catherine smiled up at him. 'It's not bad once you're out of the wind.'

A disbelieving look crossed his face, but none the less he turned down the collar of his coat as he joined her on the leeward side of the pillar. 'This is why I never learned how to ski. I hate being cold!'

Over the last few days, Catherine had been seeing a new side of Kent. She was beginning to discover that beneath the urbane façade he had always presented to her previously, he had some rather endearing human failings. Like a prospector collecting nuggets of gold, she hoarded the little bits and pieces of his personality he revealed to her, warmed by the knowledge that he was showing her a side of him that few people ever saw. 'Don't be such a baby, Kent,' she admonished him, her brown eyes teasing him. 'How are you going to stand living in Ottawa if you can't even take the almost tropical weather of British Columbia?'

He wrapped his arms around her and pulled her close. 'I guess I'll just have to take someone along to keep me warm, won't I?' He rubbed his cheek against hers and the clean male scent of him mingled with the sea air to tease her nostrils. 'Interested in the job?'

Unsure how to reply to his teasing question, Catherine leaned away from him and said, 'I never thanked you properly for inviting me to your parents'. Thank you.'

He eased his hold, leaning back against the pillar but keeping her in the circle of his arms. 'Don't thank me, Cat,' he said grimly. 'It was a disaster and you know it.' His features hardened with anger. 'I thought we would have a few days to spend some time together, enjoy each other's company. I don't think I spent five minutes alone with you after that first night.

Damn my father! I never imagined he could be so bloody unreasonable.'

'Please, Kent, don't . . .' Catherine shifted uncomfortably. 'I mean, after that first night, he never said anything to me.'

'Don't defend him, Cat,' he countered. 'He didn't have to say anything.'

Catherine looked up at him unhappily. The problem was that neither Kent nor his father was used to not having things go the way they wanted them to. Both were stubborn, arrogant men who weren't prepared to give an inch. Kent expected his father to welcome her with open arms and when he hadn't, Kent had become all the more determined that he should.

Finally Catherine said, 'Can't we talk about something else? It's not as though I'm likely ever to even see your father again, so can't you forget about it? Sometimes people just don't hit it off. I don't like feeling that I'm the cause of a quarrel between you and your father.'

Kent's mouth was set into a firm line. 'It's not your fault. I've tried to be diplomatic with him in the past, asking his opinion, his advice. I realise it's hard for him to accept that I'm thirty-three years old and no longer a child who is under his authority—but he's going to have to.' His voice grew harsh with angry emotion. 'No one dictates to me!'

His arms dropped from around her and, shoving his clenched fists into his coat pockets, Kent stalked over to the railing and stared out at the water. Catherine watched him thoughtfully. Under Kent's anger, she sensed he was hurt and a little bewildered by his father's attitude. Seeing him with his parents over the last few days, she had realised that both of them had spoiled their son. His father's money and his mother's doting attitude had combined to pave the path of his life. Whatever he wanted, he had always had, with his parents' wholehearted approval and assistance.

Catherine sighed faintly. For some reason, he had decided he wanted her, and couldn't understand why that fact alone wasn't enough to gain his father's approval. It seemed odd to think of someone like Kent having led a sheltered existence, yet in some ways he had. Disappointment, deprivation, failure—all were unknown to him. His parents, his own inherent talents and abilities, had given him a charmed life where all his desires were fulfilled, his needs met, his whims catered to.

He turned suddenly and their eyes met. 'Don't worry about him, Cat,' he said. 'I have enough faith in his integrity to believe he will eventually admit that he is wrong. He might not understand now, but once he sees how valuable you are to me, he'll come round.' A slow smile curved his lips and he held out his hand to her. 'Come on, let's go back inside where it's warm. We'll find Peter and get a cup of coffee.'

Catheine nodded her agreement; going to him and slipping her hand in his, she let him lead her back inside. She felt that Kent was being over-optimistic in his expectation that his father would have a change of heart, but she refrained from saying anything. That was the way Kent saw life: problems were made to be solved, challenges to be met. Glancing up at him, she envied his self-confidence. Too often, she knew, she retreated from the problems in her life, hiding from them instead of meeting them head on. As she was doing now. She shook that thought from her.

Peter was already in the cafeteria when they arrived and Catherine went to sit with him while Kent bought their coffee. He greeted her with a warm smile as she slid into the seat across from him.

'Was it cold out there?' he asked, his eyes appreciative as he took in her wind-flushed cheeks, the charming disarray of her hair.

'Not bad!'

Peter glanced over to where Kent was paying for the coffee. 'He still upset about his father?'

Catherine shrugged, toying with the pages of her magazine. 'I'm not sure. He said he thought he would come round later.'

'And you don't agree?'

'I don't know. It's just . . . what if he doesn't?'

'What if?' Peter returned. Seeing her expression he reached across the table and, taking her hand, gave it an encouraging squeeze. 'These things have a way of sorting themselves out, don't let it upset you.'

'Kent thinks that once his father sees how much I can help with the campaign he will accept me. I'm not so sure. What if I'm not that much help? Or even if I am, that doesn't mean Mr Latimer is going to like me any better. Kent should never have brought me with him. I don't like being the cause of a family quarrel. I think it would be better if I bowed out altogether.'

'No.' Peter was shaking his head. 'Maybe Kent is being too optimistic in his assessment of his father, but you can't walk out on him. He needs you, and not just for the campaign.'

Before Catherine could ask him what he meant, Kent came back with the coffee. For several minutes they sat sipping it, chatting amicably. Peter seemed to be determined to get all their minds off James Latimer and soon had them laughing over a ludicrous incident that had occured while he was on a road trip with the B.C. Lions.

When the laughter ended, Catherine sat back in her chair, a faint smile still curving her lips. Even in the mundane setting of a B.C. ferry cafeteria, she was conscious of Kent, of his masculinity. His thigh was a few inches from hers, his arm across the back of her chair, tempting her to lean back against it so she could experience his touch.

In a way, she was relieved they hadn't spent any time alone together over the holiday. That first night . . . what if his mother hadn't come to find her? Would they have been lovers by now? Her heart seemed to beat a little more heavily in her chest. Instinctively, she sensed Kent would be an expert lover, tender yet demanding. It would be exciting, wonderful . . . but how would she ever be able to walk away from him when he no longer wanted her? And yet might not the future heartbreak be worth it to feel his possession, just once?

Kent touched her arm and she jumped. 'Oh, I'm sorry.' A blush inched up her cheeks as she became aware that both men were looking at her with some amusement. Thank God they couldn't read her mind, though from the glint in Kent's eyes, she wondered if maybe he could. Snatching at the threads of her composure, she said quickly, 'I guess I wasn't paying attention. I was . . . thinking about the shop. You asked me something?'

It was Peter who answered. 'I was wondering about this telethon in February. Kent will be there, of course, answering phones, that sort of thing. If you could perform, it would give us great exposure. It would get your name back into the public consciousness again and that would help Kent immensely. There wouldn't be any problem getting you on it. They'd love to have someone of your stature.'

Catherine was already shaking her head. 'I thought Kent explained to you, I don't do professional engagements, even for charity. I'm sorry, Peter, but I simply can't do it.'

Peter's forehead knitted into a frown. 'Why? Listen, Cat, I heard you sing at Kent's parents' party. You were great. With rehearsal, you'll bowl them over. You're quite capable of doing this.'

'I didn't say I wasn't capable of doing it. I said I can't,' Catherine said sharply. This was not the first time a suggestion that she perform had been tendered in the last few days, and she was annoyed that Peter had brought it up yet again. In all other ways she would do what she could, but not singing. 'We discussed how I could help and I said I would accompany Kent to functions and meetings, make speeches if I have to, but I thought you understood that I can't sing professionally.'

'You keep saying you "can't",' Kent joined the conversation. 'You've said that before, why *can't* you?'

She drew a deep breath and explained, 'I'm still under contract.'

'What do you mean?'

'I mean, Rick Moss still holds my contract. I can't agree to a professional appearance without his approval. It doesn't matter whether I'm being paid for it or not, I can't do it unless he says I can.' And now Kent knew, knew that she wouldn't appear professionally again and why.

'Well, that shouldn't be a problem,' said Peter, the frown disappearing from his face. 'Just get in touch with this Moss guy and ask him to let you do this.'

'It's not that simple, Peter,' Catherine told him with a hint of exasperation. 'Rick won't let me do it without something in it for him. He didn't want me to quit.

The only way he would agree to something like this would be if I did something for him, and that means Las Vegas again. I don't want to resume my singing career.'

Deliberately, she picked up her coffee-cup and drained it, clearly indicating that the conversation had ended. Kent hadn't said anything. Was he disappointed? Trying to find a way out now he knew she wouldn't perform again?

'Cat,' Kent broke the silence that had descended over the table, 'isn't there some way you can get out of this contract with Moss? There's usually a loophole in these things.'

Catherine set down her cup abruptly. 'You don't know Rick Moss, and I do. The only loopholes are on his side, I can tell you that much. He owns Cat Devlin and has complete control over her professional life.'

'What about buying him out! How long does the contract run for?' asked Kent.

'It was a seven-year contract and I signed it shortly before Casey died, so it has two years to run. As for buying Rick out, he'd never agree,' she said with certainty, 'if for no other reason than because I walked out on him and he didn't like it.'

Before either man could reply to this, the loudspeaker announced that they were nearing the terminal and that it was time to return to their car. Catherine gathered up her belongings and stood up. She looked down at the two men, then said, 'I'm sorry. I do want to help, but I can't in that way. I . . . I just don't want to go back to singing again.' Would he understand?

Kent stood up and slipped his arm around her waist. 'I understand, Cat, but at least, can I have a look at this contract?' Catherine shrugged, then nodded. He would be wasting his time, but she doubted if he would believe her if she told him so. And he had said he understood. Perhaps he wouldn't be as upset as she had originally thought when he saw for himself how unbreakable her contract was.

Catherine jerked awake. She was breathing heavily, her heart beating double time. The bedroom was in darkness, save for the illumination from the digital clock-radio on the bedside table. Turning on her side, she looked at the time: 3.37 a.m.—she was drenched in perspiration, her nylon nightgown clinging to her, her hair damp.

Sitting up, she turned on the lamp. What had she been dreaming? Something about Casey . . . she tried to concentrate, but memory darted away like a trout, leaving only shreds of emotion. Pushing aside the blankets. Catherine got out of the bed, her actions resigned. She would not sleep again tonight, she never could after a nightmare.

In the bathroom, she turned on the taps to fill the tub and steam filled the room. Stripping off the damp gown, she stepped into the bath and leaned back, her eyes closing.

Automatically, the image of Kent came to mind. In the month since Christmas, their relationship had stabilised. The arguments that had marred it before Christmas had ceased. If anything, Kent treated her almost lovingly, even though, as yet, she had fulfilled none of her promises to work for him. When they had returned to Vancouver, Catherine had had to spend the next week working at her store. The week between Christmas and New Year was one of the busiest of the year and she was forced to spend every one of her waking hours dealing with the influx of orders for flower arrangements for holiday parties.

No sooner had New Year arrived, bringing with it a welcome respite from the demands of her business, than Catherine had been stricken by the 'flu. Though she hadn't been dangerously ill, she had been forced to spend the first ten days of the year in bed, followed by another week off work.

While Kent had naturally been disappointed, he had been kindness itself during her illness, visiting her as often as his busy schedule would permit and showering her with little gifts. Even when, as she had expected, he had been unable to find a way out of her contract with Rick Moss he hadn't reproached her, assuring her that even without her being able to sing she could still make a valuable contribution to his campaign. She had been wrong to doubt him. And in her weakened state she had cried a little at that. But still she couldn't bring herself to tell him the truth about her life and Casey's death. Finally, Kent never mentioned James Latimer, apparently unconcerned tht she had caused a quarrel between him and his father.

So why did she feel so uneasy about him? Partly, she knew that her weakened physical condition had gone a long way towards dampening her enthusiasm for helping Kent with his campaign. The by-election had yet to be called, so he wasn't exactly campaigning, and as the days passed, Catherine's dread of her emergence into the public eye grew. The anonymity of being a simple florist looked decidedly attractive as she recalled the goldfish life she had led as Cat Devlin.

More than anything, though, she admitted that the source of her unhappiness was simply that Kent was so very happy. He radiated happiness whenever she saw him, his eyes lit with pleasure, his smile never long in coming. And, as he rode his upward spiral of happiness, her own spirits plunged. He had what he wanted—Cat Devlin on his team—and where did that leave Catherine Delaney?

She had been such an idiot to fall in love with him! She wanted him to love her back, not her name, not the ghost of who she once was. She wanted him to love the flesh-and-blood reality of Catherine Delaney, not the resurrected singer Cat Devlin.

Teardrops splashed into the cooling bathwater and Catherine eased herself out of the tub and wrapped a towel around her. What did it matter that he preferred the singer to the florist? Despite his teasing offer after Christmas, it seemed unlikely that either of them would have a place in his life once he was in Ottawa— and she had promised to help him get there.

CHAPTER EIGHT

CATHERINE arrived home late from the shop. Miss Hamilton had phoned her on Kent's behalf earlier that day to ask if she was well enough to attend a dinner party with him that evening. Catherine had assured her that she was and had proceeded immediately to forget the engagement as she tried to untangle her accounting system for the bookkeeper she had finally hired. She only recalled it as she was leaving the shop and even though she hurried home, she knew she probably wouldn't be ready to leave by the time Kent called for her.

Letting herself into her apartment, she went straight to her bathroom, quickly swallowing a couple of aspirins before stripping off her clothes and stepping into the shower. Kent was due to pick her up in less than fifteen minutes. She was always careful to be ready when he arrived, but tonight that seemed impossible.

With the warm water of the shower coursing over her, Catherine thought longingly of bed. God, she was tired! She had a splitting headache and the very last thing in the world she wanted to do was go out tonight. She was stepping out of the shower when the doorbell rang. Damn him, she thought testily, why couldn't he ever be late? She quickly slipped on her robe, tying the belt as she crossed the living-room to answer the door. Throwing it open, she snapped at him before he could even greet her, 'Don't say it—I know I'm late!'

His eyes swept over her robe, a faintly puzzled look

in them as he heard the sharpness in her tone. 'Well, I didn't think you were going dressed like that,' he teased, giving her a smile he hoped would coax her into a better mood.

Instead, she cinched the belt of her robe tighter in an irritated movement as she stepped aside so he could enter the apartment. Her tone was grudging as she asked if he would like a drink while she finished dressing.

Turning to her, he nodded, inspecting her face curiously. She quickly averted it, going into the kitchen to find the bottle of Scotch she kept for visitors. She finally found it behind a box of cornflakes, and was taking down a glass when Kent came to lounge casually in the doorway. 'Ice?' Catherine asked shortly, and he shook his head frowning.

Her hand was shaking as she poured the Scotch into the glass. He came up behind her and gently took the bottle from her. Placing a hand on her shoulder, he turned her to face him, his eyes narrowing at the exhaustion written in her face. 'You look terrible. Why did you tell Miss Hamilton you could come tonight when obviously you still haven't recovered from your bout of 'flu?'

'I am recovered. I've been back at work for a week,' she protested, stung by his unflattering comments on her appearance. She pulled out of his hold and pushed her hair back from her face. 'I haven't had a chance to put my make-up on yet and I have a slight headache, that's all. I've taken some aspirin, I'll be ready in a few minutes.'

'Perhaps we should cancel tonight,' he offered, eyeing her frankly. 'You look like you could do with an early night. Everyone will understand that you don't feel up to it.'

'I'll be fine,' Catherine assured him, suddenly determined that she would. She had to start helping him some time and she didn't want to delay any longer. If she did, she might lose her courage altogether.

Leaving him with his drink in the living-room, she went to her bedroom and shut the door. Shedding her robe, she tossed it on the end of the bed. She took a cannister of talc from the dressing table and dusted her skin with the scent of Chanel No. 5 before sliding into her nylon briefs and bra. She had just pulled on her slip when a sensation of vertigo hit her. Frantically she reached out at the dressing table to steady herself, her hand knocking over a bottle of lotion with a crash.

Her bedroom door burst open behind her and Kent rushed in. 'What happened? Did you fall?'

Catherine shook her head numbly. The walls had stopped spinning about her, but she still felt odd, almost disembodied. Kent crossed the room to reach her side and took her hands in his. 'I just knocked over a bottle,' she managed to answer him. 'I'm all right.' She was unaware that her pallor and chilled hands gave the lie to her statement.

'You'd better lie down for a while.' His arm curled round her waist to lead her to the bed. Then, as her legs started to give way, he lifted her and carried her to the bed. Gently laying her on the coverlet, he sat beside her, brushing her hair back from her forehead with his hand. 'You don't seem to have a temperature,' he said softly, his blue gaze searching her face. 'When was the last time you ate?'

Her eyes shifted away from his. Had she eaten lunch today? She realised she had no idea, though she probably hadn't. No wonder she was dizzy; she had only had toast and coffee for breakfast.

She looked back at Kent. His face had taken on a harsher tone, his mouth set in an angry line. 'Have you eaten anything today? Dammit, Cat, why can't you take better care of yourself? You shouldn't have been back at work yet.' His finger touched her collarbone, then followed the clearly visible ladder of bones to the top of her slip. 'Look how thin you are! The last thing you need is to start skipping meals, especially as you've just got over being ill,' he said angrily. His hand rested on her midriff, his fingers stroking her ribs through the thin silk.

His touch was sending crazy impulses through her and she shifted uneasily. Yet she wanted him to touch her, wanted him to hold her, comfort her. She knew the instant he noticed the rapid flutter of her pulse and a slow flush crept up her face. His eyes found hers, questioning. She tried to brazen it out, pretend she wasn't affected by him, pretend she didn't know he knew it. But she couldn't hold his eyes and finally lowered her lashes to veil her own. 'I'll be fine. I was just dizzy for a moment.' She still felt dizzy, weak as though her bones had turned to rubber—but it had nothing whatsoever to do with a lack of food or her recent illness.

'Cat?' Kent's knuckles stroked her cheek. 'Cat, look at me.' She drew a shuddering breath, ignoring his order. His other hand slipped up from her waist and covered her breast, cupping her tender flesh, his thumb teasing the hardened nipple through the fine material of her lingerie. She was totally unprepared for the jolt of electricity that shot through her and her eyes flew to his face. He wanted her too—it was written as clearly as a banner headline: in his eyes, in

the set of his mouth, in the slight flush that stained his
cheekbones.

His face was coming closer to hers and she turned
her head. 'No, Kent,' she whispered. His lips touched
her jaw, his tongue traced the slender curve of her
neck. Then his mouth continued its downward
exploration, her limbs felt heavy as erotic lethargy
washed over her. They wouldn't obey her commands.
She lifted her arm to push him away and instead her
fingers curled in the dark, silken strands of his hair.

He lifted his head from her breast and his eyes
burned into hers. 'Cat, this has been inevitable for us
since the first time I kissed you,' he whispered
roughly. His mouth claimed hers, searing his brand on
her, firing her blood. His lips moved over hers in silent
demand, forcing open her own so he could explore the
softness of her mouth, his tongue sliding over the
smooth ivory of her teeth, tasting her inner lip.

Desire washed through her and she struggled
against it like an inexperienced swimmer caught in an
undertow. His hands glided over her form, sliding
under her slip to stroke her thigh. She couldn't think,
could only feel. Nothing seemed real save the
exquisite pressure of his lips on hers, the silken touch
to his hands. Her hands slipped inside his dinner
jacket, kneading the firm muscles of his back beneath
his silk shirt.

A soft moan escaped from her as he pulled away,
getting off the bed. His eyes held hers for a moment.
'You want me, Cat—and God knows I want you.'
With passion-dazed eyes she watched him remove his
jacket, hands trembling slightly as he pulled off his tie.
He smiled down at her, his blue eyes dark and hot with
primitive wanting. His shirt quickly followed the tie to
the floor, exposing a broad muscular chest covered by

a mat of dark curling hair. His stomach was flat and lean, without a sign of excess flesh.

As though bewitched, Catherine studied the body standing over her, caught in a trance of passion that paralysed her. Kent's hand went to his belt, his long, slender fingers deftly unbuckling it. As he pulled it through the loops, the reality of what was happening struck her. In one motion, she rolled across the bed to the far side, grabbing up the robe and pulling it on.

'No, Kent, we can't,' she whispered, scared of what this final commitment would do to her. She held the front of the robe shut with her arms. 'I don't want this to happen.'

For a moment he looked bewildered, then suddenly his face softened. 'Why?' he asked gently. He took a step towards her and she found she was rooted to the spot. 'I don't think you know what you want, Cat,' he said, his eyes holding hers. 'It's been building for weeks between us, don't pretend it hasn't. Tonight we're going to do something about it. We're not children, Cat.' He covered the distance between them in one stride, pulling her to him, his lips crushing hers with unrestrained ardour. He pressed her against his chest, forcing his length against her. She tried to struggle away from him, fighting herself as much as him. But he was right, so right. There was no way she could pretend to herself or to him that this wasn't what she wanted. She needed him.

He stepped forward, pinning her against the wall, all the while his mouth demanding of hers, forcing it open so he could plunder the sweetness within. Her robe opened, and she could feel the heat from his bare chest through her flimsy underwear. His heart beat hard against her and every nerve in her body responded to him, burning away the last vestiges of restraint.

In a rough movement, he snapped the narrow shoulder straps of her slip and pushed it down. Easing his hold slightly, Kent slipped his fingers between them and found the front fastening of her bra, disposing of it. His chest was hard and muscled against the softness of her bared breasts as he drew her back to him. 'See how you want me, Cat,' he whispered roughly, his palm stroking her hardened nipple.

Her fingers dug into his waist. Wild desire beat through her and she didn't resist when he lifted her off her feet and laid her across the bed. His movements were slow and seductive as he slipped the remanants of her clothing off her. 'My God, Cat, you're beautiful!' He lay down beside her, exploring her body with his eyes, his hands, his lips. She arched towards him, all resistance destroyed under the spell of the emotion that held her.

The remainder of his clothes followed hers to the floor, and she made no protest. She ached for the feel of his flesh against hers, the end to the agony of wanting. He parted her thighs to receive him and rolled on top of her. Her hands stroked the hard, muscled shoulders above her and she pulled his mouth down on hers.

The kiss was broken by her bewildered cry of pain. She tried to twist away from him, fear and pain stifling her desire. 'No, stop it!' she sobbed, struggling against him.

'What the hell . . .?' Kent froze, staring down at her. Tears were streaming down her cheeks as she looked up at him with accusing eyes. 'Cat,' he groaned, 'it's too late to stop now.' His mouth covered hers in a

warm passionate kiss. She sensed his restraint as his
fingers brushed away her tears. He was incredibly
gentle as he moved slowly against her and, as the pain
eased, the tension drained from her. Gradually the
fires that had been so brutally extinguished flared to
life, filling her with pulsing warmth until once again
she forgot everything but the exquisite sensation he
awoke in her.

Afterwards, he lay on his back to stare up at the
ceiling. Catherine turned on her side to study him, her
brain still fogged by languid passion. Tentatively, she
reached out a hand to touch him, almost afraid to
believe he was real. The last few minutes seemed like a
dream, a dream from which she didn't want to awake.

He flinched away at her touch, and quickly leapt
from the bed. His back to her, he pulled on his trousers
and shirt, not turning to face her until he was dressed.
'You should have told me, Cat,' he said bleakly. 'Put
some clothes on and come out into the living-room.
We'd better talk.' With that directive, he left the
room.

Kent was waiting for her by the window when she
went into the living-room. He had a glass of whisky in
one hand and took a large swallow from it before
indicating that she should sit down. Trying to gauge
his expression, Catherine nervously seated herself in
one of the armchairs.

'Would you like a drink?' His voice was clipped and
expressionless, but she sensed that he was holding
himself under control only with a great deal of effort.
Numbly, Catherine shook her head, refusing to look at
him. She felt terribly cold even though the apartment
was warm, and huddled deeper into her robe.

'Why didn't you tell me you were a virgin?' he asked

in a cold, controlled voice. A feeling of resentment was starting to build in her. What right had he to be angry with her? He made virginity sound like a social disease, and she glared back at him mutely. 'My God,' he swore, 'you're what? Twenty-five, twenty-six . . . I never even suspected.' He raked one hand through his hair, an expression of self-disgust marring his handsome features.

'I'm sorry if I didn't live up to your expectations but it isn't the sort of thing you can slip into every conversation,' Catherine replied in a tight voice.

He made an unintelligible noise in his throat. Though his features were still grim, his tone was softer when he spoke. 'I'm sorry, I suppose you're rather upset, but so am I. You must realise I would never have . . .'

'Look, you made your point, Kent,' Catherine interrupted him angrily. 'I'm sorry my inexperience ruined it for you. But don't worry, it won't happen again.' She was barely aware of what she was saying, but she was perilously close to tears and knew they would spill over if she stayed silent. 'I'll see if I can arrange for some lessons or something, then if it ever happens again you won't be disappointed . . .'

'Shut up, Cat,' Kent cut her off in a voice like slap. 'This isn't the time for one of your little neurotic tantrums.'

'Neurotic . . .!' Catherine exclaimed, outraged.

'Yes, *neurotic*! But just put a lid on it.' He cursed softly. 'In my book, anybody who keeps as many secrets about themselves as you do has got to have something wrong with them. Getting information out of you is like pulling teeth! Everything I know about you I've had to fight to find out. Well, this just about tears it! We're in one hell of a situation and we'd better figure some way out of it.'

Catherine took a deep breath, blinking back her tears. She hated Kent Latimer. Neurotic—how dared he say she was neurotic! She made her face expressionless, only her eyes glared at him. She'd show him who was neurotic!

'That's better,' said Kent, studying her pale, but composed countenance. 'Now, I suppose it's too much to hope that you were prepared for what happened in there.' He nodded towards the bedroom.

'Prepared?' She couldn't disguise her bewilderment.

'I didn't think so,' Kent grimaced sardonically, 'I figured that out soon after I found out you were a virgin. I think the safest thing to do is get married right away.'

'What did you say?' She blinked at him.

'I said I think we should get married ... soon ... as soon as I can arrange it.'

Catherine recoiled at the flatness in his tone and she started shaking her head. 'Kent, what are you talking about?'

'You heard me.' He stalked over to the table, picked up the bottle of Scotch and splashed more of the amber liquid into his glass.

'You mean, just because we went to bed together, you want us to get married?'

'It's the logical thing to do. Didn't your mother ever tell you where babies come from?' he asked, taking another drink from his glass. 'I didn't do anything to prevent it, and from the look of things, neither did you.'

Catherine swallowed hard. A baby—Kent's baby growing inside her. An oddly pleasant quiver ran through her, but it died quickly as she saw the expression on his face. She couldn't be having his baby. 'Just because we ... we ... th-that doesn't mean I'm pregnant.'

'But you could be, and I'm not going to take any chances.' He set his glass on the table with a loud thud.

'I'm not marrying you, Kent.' The cold deliberation with which he was planning the rest of her life hit her like a dash of cold water. 'You have to be out of your mind!' She stood up and made for the bedroom.

In two strides he was beside her, his hands going to her shoulders and roughly turning her to face him. 'You'll do what I tell you!'

She gritted her teeth, trying to control her temper. 'I think you're being ridiculous. I'm not marrying you just on the offchance I might be pregnant!'

'And if you are pregnant?'

'OK, what if I am? So what? Lots of women have babies without having husbands.' She wrenched herself away from Kent and covered her face with her hands, the impact of what could happen just hitting her. She knew all about illegitimacy, about growing up without a father. She felt sick with self-disgust—she would be just like her mother.

'I'm sure that would suit you just fine, but I'm not going to let you play the little martyr with my career.'

'What's that crack supposed to mean?'

'I mean Cat Devlin, the devoted sister, so overcome by grief when her brother kills himself in a high-powered car he couldn't control that she throws away a highly successful singing career. Who five years later is still so stricken she can't bear to talk about it, who tries to pretend that that part of her life never existed.' His voice dripped sarcasm, his eyes filled with contempt. 'Tell me something, did you really have 'flu, or was it just a last-ditch attempt to back out of your promises to me and hang on to that martyr role you're so fond of?'

Was that how it looked? Was that what he really thought? 'You know nothing, Kent, nothing about me, about Cat Devlin, about why I quit,' Catherine flung at him, not daring to accept that his assessment could be true.

'Because you won't ever tell me,' he reminded her harshly. 'But that doesn't matter any more. I've catered to your little neurosis long enough. This time my career is the one on the line and I damn well am not going to give it up.' His mouth was a thin line as he eyed her. 'It's common knowledge that we've been going out together. You end up pregnant, I'm labelled a scoundrel unless we're married. What do you think that will do to my political career?'

'Your career! That's all you think about!'

He stared at her a moment, then suddenly the anger faded from his face. He looked older, his features etched with lines of fatigue. 'It's not just my career,' he said quietly. 'I'm thinking of you, too.' He walked over to her and rested his hands gently on her shoulders. The sudden shift in mood threw her off balance, dissolving her own enmity, and she didn't resist when he pulled her into his arms. Her head rested against his chest, the steady throb of his heart beating in her ear.

'Cat,' he said presently, 'you said I know nothing about you, but you're wrong. I've watched you these past weeks, watched you stringing yourself out because you can't face what happened five years ago. I don't think you could handle something like this on your own.' She stirred, and he continued quickly, 'You'd try. I'm not saying you wouldn't. But Cat, despite the sexual revolution and all the talk about modern attitudes, there is still a stigma attached to being an unwed mother, to illegitimacy. Life wouldn't be easy for you.'

Catherine leaned against him. He was right—she, if anyone, knew that. 'Well . . . if we were sure, I suppose . . . then we would have to get married,' she conceded. They would have to—she could never let her child grow up fatherless as she and Casey had. 'But we don't have to go rushing off to do it tonight.'

'That would be the best way, Cat,' he insisted. 'There'll be eyebrows raised as it is if we become parents nine months after the wedding. And nobody would fall for that old line about it being a premature baby if we wait. Besides which, that by-election is going to be called any day now, and once the campaign is under way, we can't suddenly get married in the middle of it. It would look damn funny, especially when Junior shows up. We'll get married as soon as possible.'

If there was a baby, if they waited, some day it might find out that that was the reason they married. It would be better to do it Kent's way; that way no one would ever know. 'Yes, I suppose we have to,' Catherine whispered, knowing she was defeated.

'Fine,' Kent replied. 'I'll call the airport, see if we can get a flight to Reno or Vegas either tonight or tomorrow.'

'Why? Why can't we get married here?' Catherine protested. She didn't want to go to Nevada, not there, where Cat Devlin had lived.

'It will appear better that way—make it look like we've eloped. The press will think it's terribly romantic,' he added, with a return of irony. He went to the phone and picked up the receiver. 'Go and make us some coffee while I do some phoning—and get something to eat,' he ordered, then turned away and started to dial.

Several hours later they stepped off the plane in Las Vegas. Since agreeing to Kent's proposal, Catherine had been trapped in a numbed lethargy, her actions automatic and robot-like. She supposed she was in a state of shock, she didn't even think, her mind was shrouded in mist. Somehow she had managed to pack, but she had left everything else to Kent, letting him deal with their travel arrangements and contact Paula about the shop.

As she walked across the tarmac with Kent at her side, the glittering lights of the Strip in the distance, reality started filtering into her numbed consciousness. Within a few hours she would be married, married to Kent. The involuntary shiver that passed through her had little to do with the chill desert air in the early hours before dawn. Beginning to panic, she stumbled. Immediately, Kent's hand shot out to steady her and he retained his grip on her elbow as they made their way to the terminal.

'Kent.' She stopped suddenly as they reached the entrance to the building. The other passengers on the flight streamed around them, hurrying past them without a second glance, their thoughts on slot machines and blackjack.

'Come on, Cat.' He tugged at her elbow impatiently. 'We're in the way here.'

'No, Kent, please!' she cried desperately, trying to pull away. 'I can't. It's not too late, we don't have to go through with it.'

'We had this all out before, Cat,' he growled impatiently, drawing her through the door. 'It's far too late now, so just make the best of it.' Under the fluorescent lights of the terminal, her complexion was greyish, her eyes enormous pools of apprehension. As he relented, his tone grew gentle. 'You'll feel better after you've rested and had something to eat. We'll pick up a car here and go straight to the hotel.'

He put his arm around her waist and drew her along with him until he spotted a lounge area. Settling her into a chair, he looked down at her, frowning slightly. 'Wait here while I get the luggage and the car—and stop worrying, everything will be fine.' He smiled encouragingly at her, and walked away.

Catherine leaned her head against the back of the chair and closed her eyes. The terminal was busy even at this hour, bustling with the activity of travellers, the clang of the inevitable slot machines. If only it would be as Kent had said, that everything would be fine. She couldn't back out of it, not for either of them. She didn't want Kent hurt, and he would be if she refused to co-operate now and found out she was pregnant later. And, if she was, she knew she couldn't let the child grow up as she and Casey had, with a birth certificate with 'father unknown' and the label of bastard. Somehow she would make it work; she would have to.

CHAPTER NINE

CATHERINE heard the sound of approaching footsteps amid the background noises of the airport. Kent had been gone for several minutes, and must be returning. Opening her eyes, she sat up straighter, determined to lay her doubts aside, to forget her fears for the future.

'Cat . . . Cat Devlin! I thought it was you.' She blinked rapidly. There was no reason for her to expect to see Rick Moss just because she was in Las Vegas, yet she wasn't surprised to find him standing in front of her. For a moment she stared at him, wondering why she couldn't feel anything more than indifference.

'Hello, Rick,' she said flatly, continuing to study him. Physically, he had changed little, was still the thin wiry man with ferret-sharp features he had been five years ago. With dispassionate interest, she noted that his suit was outdated, the cuffs of his shirt slightly frayed. Rick had always prided himself on his wardrobe: the custom-made shoes, the tailored suits and silk shirts. Perhaps he's fallen on hard times, Catherine thought, wondering why the thought didn't afford her any satisfaction. Over the years her hate must have tempered, lost its intensity, until now she only felt a faint revulsion for her ex-manager.

Rick gave her an ingratiating smile and slipped into the seat next to hers. 'What brings you to Vegas? You haven't come to find me by chance? Have you finally realised how much you gave up when you walked out?' her ex-manager asked, leaning close to her and

138

watching her face avidly.

She knew better than to mention Kent to him. 'I'm just here on holiday,' she prevaricated, shifting slightly away from him.

'Cat Devlin on holiday in Las Vegas!' Rick started to laugh. 'Not likely. Darling, surely you can tell me what you're doing here?' He rested his hand on her knee in a familiar gesture. 'After all, we're old friends. Why I've always thought of you as a daughter!'

Catherine could only stare at him. How could anyone have the nerve to utter such a blatant lie? She and Casey had never been anything to Rick but a source of money. If she hadn't been aware of it before, he had proved it without a doubt when he had concealed Casey's addiction from her and everyone else. He let her brother die rather than jeopardise that precious image he had so carefully constructed for them and reaped the profits from. A feeling of nausea rose in her stomach as the old hatred for the man welled up inside her. Abruptly she stood up, unable to bear his company a moment longer. 'I don't have time to go into it now. Goodbye, Rick.'

He followed her to his feet, catching her arm to keep her with him. 'Don't run off, love. Whatever brought you here, now that you're back on your old stomping grounds, don't you see that you should never have left? It's not too late, darling. Cat Devlin can still go back on that stage. As a single you could be bigger than the Devlin kids ever were.' His fingers stroked her wrist, his smile coaxing.

At his persistence, his touch, her temper flared. 'Don't ever touch me,' ordered Catherine. Angrily she jerked her arm out of his grasp. 'Even if I wanted to, which I don't, I wouldn't go back on stage. If I sing, you're my manager. You thought you were so clever when you got Casey and me to sign that contract. You owned the Devlins, lock, stock and barrel.' Catherine suddenly laughed. 'But you can't own something that doesn't exist, can you? Casey's dead, and Cat Devlin no longer exists. You didn't realise that I would rather give up my career than be associated with a little sewer rat like you.'

A muscle twitched along Rick's jawline and his grey eyes hardened to granite. 'You always were a sharp-tongued little bitch. Have you forgotten I know where all the bodies are buried? You should be more cautious, though I'll forgive you this time. Just remember, when you change your mind I'll be waiting for you. Cat Devlin can't sing unless I say she can. Got that?'

'I'm not likely to forget it,' Catherine retorted. She saw Kent approaching them and shooting Rick one final look of distaste, turned and walked quickly towards him. When she reached him she asked quickly, 'Are you ready to go?' He nodded, his eyes questioning. Catherine knew her colour must be high, her eyes still glittering with the remnants of temper, and that Kent had noticed.

'Is there some problem, Cat?' His eyes had moved to Rick, who was standing where Catherine had left him, watching them speculatively.

Taking Kent's arm, she turned towards the door. 'No problem. Can we go?'

Outside, Kent had a rented light blue Ford LTD waiting for them. He had collected their luggage earlier and stowed it in the boot. The hotel was not far from the airport, and it was only a few minutes before they reached it. Kent had been silent during the drive, concentrating on the traffic that was heavy even at this hour. Almost before she knew what was happen-

ing, Kent was tipping the porter who had brought up
the cases and closing the door on the suite he had
arranged for them.

'Do you want a snack or something?' he asked once
they were alone.

Catherine nodded. Though she ached with fatigue
and wasn't the least hungry, she knew that if she went
to bed now, she wouldn't sleep. Seeing Rick again had
stirred up old memories, old fears. How could she
marry Kent without telling him about the past? But
where would she find the courage?

'That's probably a good idea. I noticed you didn't
eat much on the plane, Cat, and you'll probably sleep
better if you have some food inside you. I'll have the
desk send up some coffee and sandwiches.'

Since arriving in Las Vegas, Kent had been so
gentle, so solicitous. The anger that had been so
evident in Vancouver had dissolved as if it had never
been while they had flown through the stratosphere to
reach here. As Catherine watched him phone room
service, she was puzzled by his attitude. He was
accepting the situation far more calmly than she
would ever have expected. Knowing him as she did,
she knew he didn't like it when things did not go his
way, yet he had been acting almost as if he was pleased
or, at least, satisfied by this turn of events.

'You might as well freshen up while we're waiting,'
Kent suggested, breaking into her thoughts. He
crossed over to her and reaching out, pulled her gently
to her feet. 'Come on, put on your night clothes, then
you can get some sleep as soon as you've eaten.' She
looked up at him, her mouth suddenly dry. He looked
tired, faintly haggard even, but it somehow added to
his attractiveness. Lazy desire stirred within her.

'You shouldn't look at me like that,' he said quietly,

then almost reluctantly, lowered his lips to hers. Her response was instantaneous, and he gathered her closer to him, his mouth moving slowly over hers—exploratory, sensuous, tender. But there was a certain restraint too, and Catherine longed for him to deepen the kiss. She slipped her arms around him, clinging to him in unconscious appeal. She wanted him to abandon his control, to take her into the magic state they had shared earlier, where she wouldn't have to think, to worry about anything.

She caressed the firm muscles of his back and felt a tremor pass through him. Then he was putting her from him. Moving several feet away from her, he turned his back to her. His voice was low and strained as he spoke. 'Go get changed, Cat. The meal will be here soon.'

For a long moment Catherine stared at him in confusion, then turned and went into the bedroom. A quick shower and change of clothes revived her a little. Physically she was feeling much better when she rejoined Kent in the sitting-room a few minutes later. She was wearing a silky burgundy nightgown with matching negligé, yet curiously she didn't feel any embarrassment at appearing in front of Kent dressed for bed.

Room service had brought up the meal in her absence, and Kent silently handed her a cup of coffee, then indicated she should sit down. A tray of sandwiches was set out on the coffee-table and Catherine helped herself to one after sampling her coffee.

Although he had ordered the sandwiches, Kent did not join her in the meal, seemingly content to sip his coffee while she ate. He didn't look at her either, but sat staring at the floor. The tension between them grew and consequently Catherine jumped when he asked, 'Who was that man I saw you talking to at the airport?'

She cleared her throat. 'Rick Moss.'

'Your ex-business manager?'

'Yes.'

Kent grew thoughtful. 'So he's in Las Vegas, is he? Maybe that's a good thing. I'd like to see him. See if we can come up with some way of getting you out of your contract with him.' He looked at her and seeing her expression, said reassuringly, 'Don't be alarmed, Cat. I realise that you don't want to resume your career. I just don't like the idea of you being tied to him in that way.'

Catherine didn't like the idea either, but she liked the idea of Kent's talking to Rick even less. Who knew what her business manager might say to him? 'I don't think you should see him. As you say, I don't want to resume my career, so it doesn't make any difference whether I'm under contract to him or not and . . . I just don't want to have anything to do with him if I can help it.'

'I can understand that, Cat,' Kent assured her, 'but I can handle this for you without you even having to see him. After all, I'm going to be your husband. It may be an outdated attitude, but I believe a man should take care of his wife, act as a barrier between her and unpleasant situations if the need arises.' He smiled gently at her. 'You needn't worry, I'll deal with Moss for you.'

'I wish you wouldn't bother.'

'I think I should. I mean, that contract gives him a lot of control. He practically owns you as a singer.'

Catherine stood up and walked to the window, keeping her back to Kent. She swallowed with difficulty, then took a deep breath. 'I know he owns Cat Devlin, but then perhaps he has the right. He created her.'

'What do you mean—created?'

Catherine pressed her forehead against the windowpane. 'Most of what was written about the Devlins was fabrication, the result of Rick's imagination. He wanted us to have a certain image, so he invented the background to fit the image. The truth wasn't nearly as attractive.'

'And are you going to tell me the truth now?' Kent asked. Though the question was blandly spoken, Catherine sensed his quickening interest.

'I'll try. Casey and I grew up in Toronto. Our father wasn't a minister, we didn't even have a father.' Catherine shrugged. 'Our mother wasn't the type of woman men marry, if you know what I mean. Mostly she collected welfare, though sometimes she would get a job, maybe working in a bar. I didn't understand it at the time, but—she had a lot of men friends.' Catherine paused a moment, clearing her throat. 'Anyway, she walked out on us when I was thirteen and Casey was fifteen. I never missed her. Casey was always more of a parent to me than she was. After she left, we more or less brought ourselves up.'

'I don't understand,' said Kent when Catherine remained silent. 'What about the social service people? Why didn't you go to foster-homes?'

Catherine laughed softly. 'They could never catch us! We didn't want to be split up, so . . .' She lifted her shoulders.

'How did you live?'

'Oh, it wasn't bad. We had a room, the landlord didn't care how old we were as long as we paid the rent. One of Mom's boy-friends had left a guitar behind when he moved out, and Casey taught himself to play it. We'd sing on street corners and people gave us money.'

'I can't see how the authorities didn't catch up with you. What about school?' Catherine smiled faintly at the question. She could detect the incomprehension in his tone. Kent's own childhood had been so very different, filled with all the advantages his doting parents could give him.

'We didn't go to school. It's hard for someone with your background to understand. In a big city like Toronto, or Vancouver, there are hundreds of kids on their own. Runaways, or like us, abandoned.'

Kent was silent for a moment. 'Is that why you never talk about it? Because it was such an unhappy time in your life?'

He came to stand behind her and she could see his reflection in the window. She didn't want to probe the blurred features too closely, not wanting to see the pity she suspected she would find. The facts standing on their own looked bleak and stark, yet when Catherine looked back on her childhood, she remembered mainly the days spent with her brother, the bond between them.

'No, don't misunderstand,' she protested, her voice heavy with emotion. 'In many ways, I was happier then than I've ever been since. Casey and I were very close then. He . . . sheltered me, took care of me. Kids younger than I was were out there turning tricks just to get a meal, but Casey protected me from that sort of life.'

'So, where did Rick Moss come in?'

'He heard us sing and offered us the moon, so to speak. Casey . . . he was street-wise, he didn't trust Rick, but I was keen to hook up with him. Finally,

Casey gave in. It was about six months before we went to Las Vegas. Rick had us take lessons in singing, dance, diction, even the Bible. He planned an act, put it together, did everything.' Catherine turned to look at Kent, a wry smile on her lips. 'He created the Devlins.'

Kent's arms went around her and he pulled her to him. 'Why were you afraid to tell me this before? It isn't the idyllic childhood your publicity said, but it only makes me admire your brother and you far more for putting all that behind you and building decent lives for yourselves after hearing about it.'

He wasn't upset! Catherine stared up at him. 'But—what about your career? You said you needed my "untarnished image".'

He smiled slightly. 'I still have it. No one's going to dig up the truth now.'

Gently, she eased herself from him and went to stand away from him. He only knew a part of it, a very small part. She should tell him the whole thing, but she couldn't! 'Kent, I'm tired. Would you mind if I went to bed now?'

Immediately he was solicitous. 'Of course I wouldn't mind. It's been a long night.' Going to her, he slipped his arm around her waist and walked with her to the door of the bedroom where she had changed earlier. 'There's another bedroom in the suite. I'll use that one tonight so you won't be disturbed. Goodnight, Cat.' He dropped a light kiss on her temple, then held the door open for her to go inside.

Wearily, Catherine shed her robe and turned down the damask spread that covered the bed. She was bewildered by Kent's reaction. He didn't seem to mind that her image was a lie. She suspected he was pitying her after hearing about her childhood. He probably hadn't believed her when she had told him she had been happy then. But it had been the truth. Later, when their career had started to take off, the bond between her and Casey had weakened.

Catherine turned her head into the pillow, her eyes damp. How could she and Casey have drifted so far apart that she had never even suspected that he was taking drugs until it was too late? And why hadn't Rick told her? There should have been some way of getting help for Casey without incurring publicity. And even if there hadn't been, wasn't his life worth more than a career?

The next day they lunched at a pleasant café located in one of the large hotels along the Strip, and afterwards Kent drove them to the county clerk's office where the wedding was to be performed. Catherine wore a lightweight woollen suit, the colour of Devonshire cream, with a crêpe-de-chine blouse in pastel yellow. Unexpectedly, Kent had provided her with a corsage of baby roses in an unusual shade of lavender that matched the amethyst jewellery she wore.

There was a certain starkness about the wedding ceremony performed in the officious room with two rather bored-looking secretaries pressed into service as witnesses. Even when Kent slipped the heavy gold band on to her finger at the appropriate moment in the proceedings and pecked her on the cheek at the end, Catherine found it difficult to accept that they were actually getting married. They could have been transferring property or arranging for a title search in the shabby office. Nevertheless, she was relieved that he hadn't wanted to be married in one of the chapels along the Strip. While a civil ceremony might be prosaic, at least it wasn't a circus.

But she was wrong.

Catherine stopped walking, stunned, when they stepped through the front door of the courthouse. Why hadn't Kent warned her? The front steps leading to the building were crowded with people—people carrying cameras and microphones and video cameras. In other words, the press had arrived. And any chance that it was purely coincidence and that they were waiting for someone else disappeared as the air filled with shouts of 'Miss Devlin, is there any truth to the rumour . . . Why did you choose Las Vegas . . . Where . . . The honeymoon . . . Cat, are you going to be making a comeback . . .?'

She felt Kent's arm go around her waist, and she looked up at him angrily. His arm tightened and he leaned his head closer to her, saying in a low undertone, 'Don't look like that, Cat. I didn't call them, but since they're here, we have to face them. Come on, smile!'

Fitting his own actions to the words, he looked out at the crush of reporters, a practised smile on his face. Catherine had no choice but to follow suit, wincing slightly as flashbulbs exploded in front of her. Then Kent was urging her down the steps, his patient smile never faltering as he repeated with the monotony of a broken record. 'No comment, my wife will be issuing a statement later,' in answer to the bombarding questions.

Fortunately, the car was parked nearby and though the press followed after them like the train of a bridal gown, Kent managed to install her in the passenger seat and take his own place behind the wheel without her having to say one word to the reporters.

Catherine sat huddled in her seat, staring mutinously out of the window as Kent drove them towards the hotel. For a few moments he negotiated the traffic in silence, then finally he said impatiently, 'Stop blaming me, I didn't call them. At least give me credit for being sensitive enough not to spring something like that on you without warning.'

'Well then, how did they find out?'

'How should I know?' Kent snapped. 'Look, Cat, stop getting yourself in a stew about it. They were going to find out eventually. Sure, it would have been nice if we could have planned it, been prepared, but it hasn't worked out that way so there's no point working yourself up.'

'I just wish we could have avoided them,' Catherine said sulkily. She knew she was being childish in taking her anger out on Kent, but the reporters had shaken her. Now that she thought about it, she had a pretty good idea who had informed the press. She wasn't sure how Rick had found out about the wedding, but he knew she was in town. Besides, just the number of reporters who seemed to think she was contemplating a comeback suggested that someone had given them the idea. Damn Rick! If he thought he could use public pressure to force her back into working for him, he could think again.

Catherine sent Kent a surreptitious glance. In profile, his features looked set and she knew he was annoyed with her. He had a right to be. When she had seen all those reporters she had almost panicked. He had got her out of a tricky situation and all she had done was snipe at him. 'I'm sorry, Kent,' she said softly. 'I know you didn't call them. It was probably Rick. The way his mind works, he probably figured he could get me to do a performance if the press applied some pressure.'

Kent glanced at her and quickly turned off the main

thoroughfare on to a side-street. Pulling the car to the side of the road, he turned to face her, drawing her into his arms. 'Don't take this so hard, Cat. Rick's not going to be able to force you back to work. I'll handle him. As for the press ...' He paused, his arms tightening around her. 'I wish I could tell you that you'd never have to face them again, but I can't. I've worked too long and too many people depend on me to throw away my career now. The public is always going to be curious about us: me, because I'm a politician, you, because you're Cat Devlin. But I can promise you this, Cat.' He eased her away from him and stared intently into her eyes. 'I'll do everything in my power to protect you. We'll play down your life as an entertainer, we'll let them know that you're Mrs Kent Latimer now, my wife, and that the past is dead. I won't let them probe those old wounds, darling.'

Suddenly she could no longer meet his eyes, and buried her face in his shoulder. He made her feel safe and protected, and she hadn't told him everything. 'Kent,' she whispered in a muffled voice, 'you should know that ...'

'No, Cat,' he interrupted her gently. His hand under her chin, he lifted her face to his. Briefly his lips touched hers. 'Some day, maybe, we'll talk more about it. Not today, though, not on our wedding day. Today is a day for the future, not the past.' Once more he kissed her tenderly, a gesture of reassurance, then he released her to make the drive back to the hotel.

Another pack of news-hungry reporters was lying in wait for them in the lobby of their hotel, but once again Kent took charge and brought Catherine through the horde unscathed. A magnum of French Champagne and six dozen red roses waiting for them when they returned to their suite, courtesy of Rick

Moss, confirmed Catherine's suspicion that he had tipped off the press.

The heavy scent of the flowers that filled the suite set off a surge of homesickness in Catherine. Rick probably thought it wouldn't be long before he could afford his ostentatious gift.

Kent went over to inspect the champagne, and lifting the bottle out of the ice bucket, he whistled softly as he read the label. 'Very impressive!' He turned to where Catherine had settled on the sofa. 'He must want you to go back to work pretty badly.'

She shrugged, then said, 'He probably just has itchy feet.'

'Has what?'

'Itchy feet. Casey and I used to joke about Rick's itchy feet. One of the little perks of being the Devlins' manager was that he got to take a lot of trips. He was always jaunting off to Mexico or Montreal, supposedly to gather material for our act. He'd find songs for us written in Spanish or French and bring them back and have them translated for us to sing. Though the material wasn't new, the melodies were unfamiliar to the English-speaking market. In theory I guess It was a good idea.'

Kent eyed her interestedly. 'By that last remark, I take it it didn't work out that well in practice.'

'Most of the stuff he brought back was garbage, songs we would never use or that sounded ridiculous when translated,' Catherine told him.

'I'm surprised he kept doing it if you couldn't use the material.'

'Like I said, itchy feet,' she drawled. 'The trips were a business expense, so they came out of our income.'

Kent's mouth firmed slightly and he glanced from the champagne to the roses. Finally he said. 'I know you don't want me to, but I think I ought to have a talk with him, find some way of getting you out of your contract with him?'

He looked dissatisfied when she firmly shook her head, but nevertheless dropped the subject. He returned the champagne to the ice bucket and said, 'I think it would be better for us to have dinner up here tonight—avoid our friends in the lobby. If you want to change, I have a couple of phone calls to make, then we'll try out friend Rick's champagne. I was supposed to meet my dad in Victoria today and I'm afraid I forgot all about it. Besides, I want to let him know what's going on so he'll be prepared for when the news breaks.'

Somehow Catherine had managed to forget all about about James Latimer in the last twenty-four hours. He hadn't liked her as Kent's girl-friend, how was he going to react when he found out she was now his son's wife? At the contemplation of yet another problem, Catherine felt inordinately weary. She stood up slowly to go into the bedroom to change. Kent was already at the phone and he smiled encouragingly as she walked out of the room. If she didn't know better, she would almost be tempted to think he was glad about their sudden marriage.

In the bedroom, she slipped off her suit jacket and carefully hung it in the wardrobe. Next, she removed the amethyst clip earrings she had worn for the wedding and started to unclasp the gold chain from around her neck that supported the matching pendant. The clasp was stiff and after fumbling with it for a moment, she tried to pull it around to the front to get a better view of it. Unfortunately, it had become tangled in a loose thread from her blouse and wouldn't move. She would have to get Kent to help her.

Her footsteps were muffled by the deep carpeting and as she had neglected to pull the door completely shut, she entered the sitting-room without Kent's being aware of her presence. He was still on the phone, his back to her, and not wanting to interrupt, Catherine remained by the bedroom door until he was finished.

Though not intentionally eavesdropping, she couldn't help overhearing his side of the conversation. She heard him struggling to describe the outfit she had worn to get married in, then almost laughed out loud when he finally said in exasperation, 'Mom, I don't know what kind of material it was! It was yellow and it was soft. Now, let me talk to Dad.'

The conversation with his father was less entertaining, mainly because Kent said very little and Catherine was too far away to hear the other side of it. Suddenly, though, Kent tensed, then said harshly, 'I am well aware of the benefit to my career of choosing the "right" woman for my wife.'

He fell silent, listening to the man on the other end of the line, then snapped, 'I know all I need to know about her . . . No, I don't think it was strange that she ended her career when her brother died.

'. . . I don't know what you're trying to imply, but she's your daughter-in-law now, so you'll just have to accept it . . .' The knuckles of the hand holding the receiver whitened. 'It was straightforward, a car accident, no scandal in that. They were very close and as far as her singing now, I explained . . .'

CHAPTER TEN

CATHERINE closed the bedroom door silently behind her, shutting out the phone conversation. Why had she ever listened? No scandal! The scandal was there all right, waiting like some ghastly creature trapped in a locked box. She and Rick had covered up how Casey had died, making it look like a car accident, but other people must have known about the drugs, even if she hadn't. Casey hadn't lived in a vacuum. What if one of them decided to let that monster out?

She felt sick. Why hadn't she told Kent the whole truth last night? She hadn't wanted to discuss it because it was like an unhealed wound inside her and she wanted to avoid the pain that probing would bring. It just hadn't occurred to her that the secret of the scandal from her past was not just known to her.

Damn Rick! What could she do now? He had closed the one door open to her. They could have had the marriage annulled, called the whole thing off. It was too late now, everybody knew they were married. The embarrassment of having the bride walk out straight after the wedding would create its own scandal.

Raising trembling hands to her face, Catherine knew she did not have the courage to tell Kent about Casey. The secret had been safe for years, she had to pray that it would remain that way.

She looked down at the pendant, realising she had

been standing by the door for some time. Kent would be wondering what had happened to her. She didn't want him to know she hadn't even started changing yet, so she grasped the amethyst teardrop and gave it a sharp tug. The fine chain parted and Catherine removed it from around her neck and tossed it on to the dresser. Quickly shedding her clothes, she took out an emerald-green crêpe evening gown from the closet and pulled it on. Sparing only a moment to touch up her make-up, she quickly brushed her hair, then fastened her diamond necklace around her throat. Slipping on the matching earrings and finding her shoes, she was ready to return to the living-room.

Kent was still standing by the phone when she entered, a brooding expression on his face as he stared at the instrument. Hearing her come in, he turned to look at her. His features were etched into bitter lines and the blue shadow of his beard stood out starkly against his abnormally pale complexion.

The silence hung between them like an acrid mist. Catherine could feel her heart thumping in her chest and she nervously twisted the gold band that adorned her finger. Finally, she couldn't take the silence any longer and, moistening her dry lips, she asked, 'Your father . . . was he terribly upset?'

'He's not ordering any brass bands to welcome us home,' Kent snapped, and Catherine flinched. Seeing her stricken look, he rubbed the nape of his neck with one long-fingered hand. Looking up at her again, his eyes were softer. 'I'm sorry, I had no right to snarl at you. He was mad. I know I should have expected him to be, but I don't know . . .' he shrugged, 'I thought once the deed was done, he would accept it. I know what people say about him, that he's strong-willed, ruthless even, but that's the way he had to be in business. Our family life . . . he's been a strict parent and perhaps more remote than other fathers, but I've always respected him, felt that he cared. I thought I understood him. I'm beginning to think I've never known him at all.'

Catherine read the pain and disillusionment in his eyes before he turned his back to her. This whole mess was her fault. She should never have let Kent talk her into marrying him. Her hands fluttered uncertainly in front of her. She wanted to go to Kent, to comfort him, but her own sense of inadequacy kept her rooted to the spot. She should never have entered his life.

Kent turned around again, giving her a faint smile. 'I'm sorry, Cat. This has been a hell of a day for you, hasn't it?' Crossing the room to her, he took her hands in his and looked down at her. 'You deserve so much more than I've been able to provide. I can only say that I'll try to make all your tomorrows better than this day has been.' A tender light gleamed in the depths of his eyes and he gently stroked her hands. 'We made some promises this morning and I want you to know that I'll stand by them. Maybe I'm old-fashioned, but I think marriage is for keeps. I don't believe in divorce at the first sign of trouble. We'll both have to work at making a go of this. If there are problems, we can overcome them if we try. And we will try, won't we, Cat?'

Catherine lowered her lashes, hiding the shame in her eyes. He didn't know all the problems they faced, he didn't know that some could never be overcome. As the evening progressed, so did her guilt. Kent was trying, trying very hard. He smiled often, teased her gently over the meal sent up by room service. He raised a glass of Rick's champagne, toasting her with fulsome compliments. And as the hours passed, her guilt gained momentum. Just occasionally, she would catch a bleak look crossing his face, a note of resigned dejection in his eyes. She knew he was thinking of his father, of the rift between them—a rift she had caused.

They were seated on the sofa, Kent's arm around her shoulder as they sipped coffee and liqueurs. Kent moved his hand, gently tracing a pattern along her arm and up her shoulder. 'You have nice skin. It feels like warm velvet under my fingertips.' The arm tightened around her, drawing her closer to his side. He reached out and took away her coffee-cup, setting it on the side-table before turning back to her.

As she saw his head move towards her, she moved away, jumping off the sofa and going to stand several feet away, her back to him. When he looked at her with warmth, with tenderness, all she could see was her own dishonesty.

'Let's go out for a while,' she said, her voice unsteady.

'Out?'

She turned around then, smiling at him with effort. 'Yes. Let's go downstairs to the casino. I feel like playing blackjack. Casey and I used to play sometimes after our show finished. It's a lot of fun. I haven't played for years.' The enthusiasm she had tried to inject into her voice held a note of desperation and she saw him frown. But she had to get away from this room, away from Kent, before guilt drove her into saying things best left unsaid.

'It's almost midnight, Cat.' Kent was watching her closely, taking in the little nervous gestures, the hands that were clasped tightly together, the eyes that wouldn't meet his.

'Well, you know how it is in Las Vegas. Time doesn't matter.' Kent had risen from the sofa and was coming towards her. Nervously, Catherine babbled on, 'Don't worry, Kent. I'm not going to lose all your money. I know how to play. Casey and I had a system. You have to watch what the dealer's up card is——'

'You don't have to be afraid of me, Cat,' Kent said gently, putting his hands on her shoulders.

'Afraid?'

'You've been tense all night ... Cat on a hot tin roof,' he teased. 'The other night was the first time for you, but it will be better this time. I promise you. Tonight's our wedding night, love. I don't want to spend it playing cards ...' He lowered his head, his lips seeking hers. For a moment Catherine resisted the caress, unyielding and impassive in his arms. Then slowly she relaxed, allowing her emotions free rein as she responded to the tender asking in his touch. The guilt would return, but for now, she seized selfishly on the physical love he offered, letting desire blot out the nagging ache of her conscience.

She was breathless when finally he lifted his head and smiled down at her. Smoothly he lifted her off her feet and automatically she linked her arms around his neck. His eyes were soft blue and, as she stared into them, a knot of pain tightened in her stomach. He deserved so much more than she could offer. He deserved trust and honesty, but she was too weak to give them. Tears pricked her eyelids and she closed them as he carried her into the bedroom.

Curiously enough, the next few days passed pleasantly. Kent arranged for them to be away from Vancouver for a week and though he suggested they might want to leave Las Vegas for somewhere else, Catherine found she was enjoying her stay. In a sense, Vegas was almost her home town. She had lived there for five years during her singing career and knew the out-of-the-way places and local beauty spots that tourists rarely saw and enjoyed sharing them with Kent. Inevitably, she was occasionally recognised, but found that a hastily scribbled autograph satisfied most fans.

As the roses lost their pristine freshness and Rick Moss made no attempt to contact her, the tension gradually eased out of her. She still felt guilty for not telling Kent about Casey's death, but for the most part she simply avoided thinking about it.

They had been married for four days when they returned late one afternoon to their suite in the hotel. They had spent the day on the ranch of one of Catherine's friends from the old days. When Anthony Graves had called, asking her to visit him, she had been reluctant to go, afraid he might say something about Casey in front of Kent. She hadn't wanted to hurt Tony's feelings though, or make her excuses with Kent in the same room as she took the call, so she had finally agreed. She needn't have worried. The comedian seemed to sense that Catherine didn't want to talk about old times and quite happily kept the conversation on what they were doing with their lives now.

'Are you going to rest for a while?' asked Kent as he inserted the key into the door of their room. 'We'll be up late if we're going to Tony's midnight show.'

'I think I will.' She hesitated, then, 'You don't mind, do you—going to see the show, I mean?'

'Of course not,' he assured her. 'I'm looking forward to it. I liked Tony.' He suddenly grinned at her. 'I'll admit, though, that I liked him a lot better after I'd met him.'

Catherine looked blank and he laughed, slipping his arm about her shoulders and hugging her. 'When you suggested we go visit him, I was afraid you were taking me to meet an old flame.'

'Tony? He's practically old enough to be my grandfather!'

'I know,' he said with satisfaction, pushing open the door to the suite and propelling her through it. He stopped abruptly. James Latimer was standing in the centre of the lounge. 'Dad! What are you doing here?'

'I came to talk to you.' Though he had spoken to Kent his black gaze rested on Catherine, and her blood suddenly cooled.

'I'm on my honeymoon, Dad,' Kent reminded him in a light tone that was still puzzled. 'Couldn't it have waited?'

'I don't think so.' Beneath James's carefully controlled voice lurked pure rage. His eyes bored into Catherine's like diamond drill bits and he said, 'Have you told him what you and that little worm are up to yet?'

Catherine stared back at him, then horror slowly darkened her eyes. Rick—she hadn't heard from Rick these past few days. He hadn't even tried to see her.

That wasn't like him. What had he been doing?

Kent turned his head to look at her and saw that the colour had seeped from her face. He quickly looked back to his father. 'What are you talking about?' he demanded.

The smile that twisted his lips was cruel and his eyes never left Catherine's face. 'Shall I tell him? Shall I tell him how the little gold-digger he was stupid enough to marry is trying to get her claws into me? Shall I tell him how your lover is trying to blackmail me?' The control left his voice as it rose in volume.

There was more than just anger in James Latimer's face, there was triumph written in his harsh features: he thought his opinion of her had been vindicated. Catherine pulled herself together.

'It's Rick, isn't it? What does he want?'

'Don't pretend you don't know!' snarled James Latimer.

'I *don't* know!' Catherine shouted, erupting with anger. She glared at the two men, then focused on Kent. His face was as pale as her own and his eyes were bewildered. Abruptly, her anger drained away. 'Whatever your father says, Rick Moss is not my lover and never has been. I hate Rick Moss. I would kill him if I could!'

For several seconds she held Kent's eyes, then she saw him take a deep calming breath and turn to his father. 'I want to know what's happened.'

James Latimer's eyes flicked over her with contempt before he gave his son his attention. 'Rick Moss came to see me last night. He's got some pictures. He'll sell them and the negatives to me for one hundred thousand dollars. We'll have to give it to him. If they ever became public, you'd be finished in politics.'

Catherine saw Kent swallow convulsively and if possible, grow even more pale. 'What sort of pictures?' he asked huskily.

His father laughed derisively. 'Not porn, if that's what you're worried about.' He shot Catherine a scornful look. 'If that was it I would let her hang. No, in some ways this is worse. These pictures are of her brother when he died, of his body, and she's in them.'

Kent frowned and shook his head. 'I don't understand. Casey Devlin died in a car accident. His body was burned beyond recognition.'

Before Mr Latimer could respond, Catherine said quietly, 'That isn't what happened: we just made it look like that. Casey ... Casey died from a drug overdose. I didn't want anyone to know, so I let ... I let Rick talk me into covering up what happened.' She put her hand over her eyes, willing herself not to cry. She hadn't known about the pictures; she hadn't been aware of Rick's taking them. She wasn't surprised, though. He must have been saving them all these years just waiting for an opportunity to tear her life apart.

'In the pictures, she's standing with the body, holding a needle and a packet of white power. It's pretty obvious what happened,' James Latimer elaborated. 'I——'

'When does Moss want the money?' Kent cut his father off in a flat voice.

'The day after tomorrow, delivered to him here in Las Vegas: cash, small bills.' James smiled wryly. 'He wants it in US dollars.'

'You can go back to Victoria, then. I'll take care of it.'

'I can afford it more than you can. I'll pay him. That's what fathers are for.' There was a sarcastic edge to James's tone.

Kent's temper snapped. 'I said I would take care of it!' Seeing his father's expression, he said, 'Look, I'm not some seven-year-old who's put a ball through the neighbour's window and has to have Daddy put it right for him. I've grown up, even if you don't want to admit it. I'm a man and I'll take care of my own life.'

'Well, you've done a fine job so far—letting this little tramp get her hooks into you.' Mr Latimer tossed his head derisively in Catherine's direction. 'If you wanted her, you should have just taken her—you didn't have to be fool enough to marry her!'

Catherine held her breath as Kent clenched his fists white-knuckled by his side. She saw him make a slight movement towards his father and she quickly stepped between. 'Stop it, Kent! I won't have you fighting over me!'

'I'm not going to let him talk about you like that!' rasped Kent.

Catherine clutched at his arm. 'Please, Kent, just forget it.' She could feel the tensed muscles of his forearm and met his eyes with pleading in her own. 'Please, don't,' she begged.

After a slow minute of agonised waiting, he slipped his free arm about her shoulders and turned her to face James Latimer. 'For Cat's sake—and for Mom's—I'm going to pretend you never said what you did. Whether you like it or not, Cat's my wife and you'd better get used to the idea. Now, I think we should check with the airport about getting you a flight out of here.'

'Don't bother,' James Latimer retorted, stalking past him to the door. 'I'll take care of it myself.' Wrenching open the door, he went through it and slammed it behind him.

'I'm sorry,' Catherine broke the silence that followed his exit. 'I didn't . . .' She trailed off at the look of anguish on Kent's face.

'Can't we talk later?' he interrupted harshly, then in a gentler voice: 'I need some time to take this all in.' With one hand, he kneaded the muscles at the back of his neck, then looked over to her. 'I'm going out for a while. I'm sorry, I know I shouldn't walk out on you like this, but right now . . . I don't know what to say to you . . . I don't know what I think. I know you didn't put Moss up to this.' He laughed bitterly. 'I trust you . . . even if you've never trusted me enough to tell me about your brother. But . . . I've got to have a little time.'

The quiet click of the door closing behind him sounded deafening in the silent suite. He wanted a little time, she thought bitterly, so he wouldn't say something precipitate. He hadn't taken that time when he insisted she marry him, so he must have learned something from that mistake. How could he help but regret that she had ever come into his life?

Blinded by tears, she made her way to the sofa and wept uncontrollably for several minutes. Finally, the tears were spent and she lay exhausted against the damp cushion of the couch. As her emotional crisis passed, her thoughts grew clearer. As Kent could not let his father pay for his mistake in marrying her, she could not let Kent pay for her past. She would have to pay Rick herself. Fortunately, in that stunned lethargy in which she had packed, she had tossed in her jewellery case without simply sorting out a few pieces to take with her. She would get it from the hotel safe and Rick would have to accept that in lieu of the Latimers' money.

Getting to her feet, she went to the bedroom to change and wash the tears from her cheeks. It shouldn't be hard to find Rick. He didn't seem to have changed much over the years, so he probably still frequented the same hangouts.

Three hours later, Catherine stood in the hallway of one of the upper floors of Caesar's Palace steeling herself to knock on the door before her. Thinking of the worn suit Rick had been wearing when she saw him at the airport, she decided he wasn't wasting any time before enjoying his anticipated wealth. The bartender at the watering hole where she had enquired about Rick's whereabouts had told her he had moved here only this morning from a far less opulent dwelling.

She raised her hand and knocked, half hoping no one would respond, but the door opened after only a brief respite. 'Why, if it isn't Cat Devlin!' Rick beamed at her, then flung his arm back in a gesture for her to enter. 'And to what do I owe the pleasure of this visit, darling?' he asked as she had silently walked past him.

'I think you can guess, Rick,' she said flatly, turning to face him as he leaned negligently against the now closed door.

His eyebrows lifted in his weasel-like face and he

said, 'Can I? Perhaps you're calling on old friends tonight?'

'This isn't a social call and you know it!'

He pursed his lips mockingly at the hardness in her tone and straightened. 'Well, even if it's business, we can still make ourselves comfortable. Please, take a seat. I'll call room service and have them send up drinks. Champagne, I think. It's been such a long time since we discussed business together, we should celebrate the occasion.'

He started towards the phone and Catherine remained where she was, saying coldly, 'I don't want anything from you but those pictures and the negatives.'

Rick gave her a guileless look. 'Now what pictures would those be?'

'You know damn well what pictures!' She temporarily lost control over her temper and had to struggle to regain it. 'I want them. Oh, don't worry . . . I know I'll have to pay for them. But I want them, and I don't want the Latimers involved. This is between you and me.'

The ingenuous façade dropped from him like a cloak as his eyes grew sly. 'You know what I'm asking for them?'

'One hundred thousand dollars.'

'Cash,' he reminded her with a sarcastic smile.

Catherine mentally crossed her fingers before saying, 'I don't have the cash, but I have my jewellery.' She withdrew the case she had taken from the hotel safe earlier and laid it on the table beside her. 'You know the jewellery, Rick. You can have it in exchange for the pictures and the negatives. It's worth twice what you're asking.'

He gave her a considering look, then asked softly, 'Is it, Cat?'

'You know it is, Rick. You complained enough about the cost when Casey was buying it for me. I only sold one set after he died—the emeralds. All the other pieces are there.'

Casually, he walked over to the table and picked up the case. Opening it, he lifted out the pearls and inspected them. As she watched him finger the smooth orbs she felt almost as though he were violating her. Even if he refused to accept them, she doubted that she could ever bear to wear them again. 'They're very nice,' he said after a moment. 'It's all nice—but it ain't worth no hundred grand.'

'That jewellery is worth twice that,' she reiterated, her anxiety mounting when she couldn't control the tremor in her voice. She mustn't let him know she was afraid he wouldn't accept them.

'Sorry, kid, no way.' He shrugged and dropped the pearls back into the case before setting it down again.

'I want those negatives, Rick,' Catherine demanded through clenched teeth.

He smiled maliciously. 'And you'll have them.'

She stared at him warily. 'What do you mean?'

'You'll get the negatives when you've worked out your contract. And I mean singing, no more hiding up in Canada. I want you back on that stage. In exchange, I'll give you the pictures at the end of the two years.' Unconsciously, Catherine was shaking her head. 'It's that,' said Rick harshly, 'or I release the photographs to the press.'

'What if I could get the money?' she asked, a note of

desperation in her tone.

He shook his head firmly. 'Not now. I've changed my mind.' He laughed. 'Bet you thought that was only a woman's prerogative, didn't you? This is the only way I'll ever let you have them.'

'I can't.'

Rick stared at her through narrowed eyes, then said casually, 'Then I guess you'd better go tell that new husband of yours what you've decided. You might mention that if he's curious about the photos, he'll be able to have a look at them in the morning papers.'

'You're bluffing!'

'Am I? You know the police might even get interested in why you covered up your brother's death like that. They might even wonder if he was really dead when you pushed that car over the cliff.'

'He was dead, you know he was. And besides, it was your idea to cover up what really happened. You have as much to lose as I do if those photos are ever publicised.'

He tutted, shaking his head. 'No, I don't. I can produce twenty witnesses who will swear I was having a lucky streak at the tables that night. I wasn't anywhere near the desert. It was all you and Brian. By the way, I'll explain that he took the pictures and gave them to me just recently.'

It was like a nightmare, growing worse and worse and yet she knew she wouldn't wake up from it.

'So what'll it be, kid?' he asked.

Her mouth was dry and she moistened her lips with her tongue. 'I'll work out my contract,' she whispered.

'Fine.' He smiled at her. As she reached out to pick up the jewellery case preparatory to leaving, his hand touched her arm. She pulled back as though burnt. 'Just leave them, Cat. They may not be worth a hundred grand, but they're enough to get us started again. You'll need costumes, a band, we'll have to find a place to rehearse—not to mention publicity. I'll call you at your hotel when I have things arranged.' He walked to the door and held it open for her. 'Goodnight, Cat. Sweet dreams!'

CHAPTER ELEVEN

'WHERE the hell have you been?' Kent's angry voice broke over her like a cresting wave as she walked into their suite. Catherine stopped, unable to say anything for a moment. She was near the end of her endurance, feeling that if the earth suddenly opened and swallowed her, she would welcome it as an escape from the purgatory of the last few hours—the next two years.

'Do you realise I've been half out of my mind worrying about what happened to you?' Kent demanded. He was in his shirt-sleeves, his collar undone and his tie askew. As she stared at him mutely, she noted his complexion had an odd greyish tinge to it. 'I wasn't even gone an hour and when I got back you'd disappeared. Maybe I was being selfish to leave like that, but you have to understand, that was one hell of a thing to have dumped on me all at once. I didn't want us to get into an argument over it. We're in a damnable mess and fighting with each other about it isn't going to help. That's why I figured I'd better take a few minutes to get a hold of myself before we talked.' He was breathing heavily as he looked at her and his next words suggested that he had not gained total control over his emotions during his respite from her. 'You never even gave me a clue something like this could come up. I thought . . . I thought, especially after you told me about your childhood the other night, that it was only because you were so close to your brother that you couldn't bear talking about him, about your career. I never imagined he was a drug addict.'

Catherine averted her head, biting her lip. 'I'm sorry,' she said in a small voice.

'I'm your husband. I wish you could have trusted me.'

'I'm sorry,' she repeated inadequately. 'I suppose your father . . .'

'Leave my father out of this. You're as bad as he is,' Kent accused impatiently. 'This is between you and me . . . he doesn't come into it. You're *my* wife, not his. You should have told me, but whether you did or not has nothing to do with my father.' She couldn't think of one word in reply, and finally he continued, 'Anyway, as I said before, I don't want to get into an argument over this. Where have you been?'

The phone rang. 'That'll be Peter,' he explained as he strode over to it. 'Kent Latimer here,' he said into the receiver, then after a brief pause, 'Look, Peter, I'll get right to the point. You know that letter I made out a few months ago giving you my power of attorney? I want you to go to my office tomorrow morning before the markets open and take it and my portfolio from the safe. As soon as the exchanges open, I want you to start selling off my stock.' His voice rose as he cut off speech from the other man. 'Look, Peter, I need one hundred thousand dollars—US—and I need it fast . . . No, of course I haven't been gambling . . . and yes, I know I'll be taking a loss on some of it . . . I can't explain over the phone. Just do it, then bring it to me . . . Well, yes, try to hang on to my stock in Latimer's, but sell it if you have to. I need the full hundred thousand.'

'No, Kent!' Catherine ran to him, grabbing his arm. 'You can't . . . besides, you don't need to. I've taken care of Rick . . . I saw him tonight. We don't need the money now—we don't need it!'

Kent stared at her, a frown settling on his brow, then he said quickly into the phone, 'You're at your apartment, aren't you? I'll call you back in a minute . . . something's come up here.'

He set the receiver back into its cradle, and turning to her, asked slowly, 'What are you talking about? Why don't we need the money any more?'

Catherine hesitated. Then she said, 'I went to see Rick tonight. I wanted to get the pictures from him.'

Kent swore softly. 'You shouldn't have gone by yourself. He might be dangerous. You don't know.' He pushed his hair back off his forehead in a distracted gesture. 'You must have gotten the pictures, though?'

'No,' Catherine admitted softly.

'No? Then what happened?'

She couldn't meet his eyes. 'We made a deal. He'll give them to me when I've . . . I've worked out my contract with him.'

'When you've *what*? Are you out of your mind? You can't go back to work for him . . . unless, of course, that's what you want,' Kent added in a hard voice.

'Of course that's not what I want!' Catherine cried. 'But it's the only way. He said the only way he would let me have those negatives was if I finished my contract with him. I gave him my jewellery, but he said it wasn't enough.'

'But he kept it?'

'Yes, to pay the expenses of putting a show together again.'

Once again, Kent swore, and Catherine winced. 'Are you sure you don't want to go back to work for him?'

'You know I don't,' she said tearfully.

He went to her and wrapped her in his arms. 'Don't cry, Cat. You don't have to go back to him. We'll pay him.'

'You don't understand, Kent. He said he wouldn't take the money now. He insists that I work for him.'

He placed his finger under her chin and tipped her face up to his. Gently, his mouth covered hers, then he lifted his head away. 'I'm sure he'll take the money once we get it together. Now let me call Peter back so he can get to work on it.'

Catherine backed away from him, shaking her head. 'I don't want you to. I don't want to work for him, but I know him and if he says it's the only way, he won't change his mind. You'll be wasting your time and your money. Even if he takes it, I don't think he would give up the pictures, now.'

'Trust me to deal with him. I think he'll take the money once we have it for him.'

'No, he won't ... besides, it's not really your problem, it's mine. Casey was my brother, and I'm the one who should never have tried to cover things up. I don't want you getting involved.'

Some of the colour left his face as she spoke and he kept his eyes averted. 'I see,' he said in a clipped voice. 'Forgive me. I thought that as I'm your husband that made your problems mine. Obviously you don't agree.' His mouth twisted bitterly and he suddenly looked her full in the face, his blue eyes darker than she had ever seen them. 'Even if we don't agree on what a husband's role in a marriage is, I think you have to accept that a parent has certain responsibilities. Have you forgotten you might be pregnant? Isn't that why we got married in the first place? It's even more of a possibility now ... we haven't exactly been playing poker every night since we got here! I'm calling Peter and having him get the money. If you think I'm interfering in your affairs, then I'm sorry, but I'm not doing it for you. I'm doing it for the baby who might be in jeopardy if you insist on resuming your career.'

Catherine felt as though he had kicked her. 'I understand.' She turned quickly so he wouldn't see her tears and went into the bedroom.

'Boy, that sure looks like an awful lot of money when it's all in cash like that,' commented Peter Castle as he stared mesmerised into the open briefcase filled with stacks of bills.

'It *is* an awful lot of money,' Kent returned drily, his own eyes resting on the piles of green paper.

For Catherine's part, she avoided looking at the money. Just thinking about it made her feel sick. It was all so pointless! If Rick took it at all, he would just say it was to cover the expenses of putting her act together. He wouldn't give up the negatives: she knew that as certainly as she knew her own name. Rick loved living in the limelight, being the man behind the star.

Peter and Kent were discussing the logistics of delivering the money to Rick and she tried to shut out their voices. She and Kent had barely spoken to one another since their argument the night before last. She had overheard Peter telling him that he had taken a beating on the stock that had been sold to raise the money. That made her feel even worse about it all.

There was a knock at the door and Catherine saw the two men quickly exchange glances. They were edgy, but then who could blame them? It wasn't every day one had a hundred thousand dollars in cash lying around.

'I'll get it,' said Kent, going to the briefcase and snapping it closed. He picked it up and handed it to Peter. 'Maybe you'd better wait in the bedroom with this.'

'Good idea,' he agreed, accepting the case. Kent waited until the bedroom door had closed behind him before going to receive the caller.

'Can I help you?' Kent asked in a choked voice after opening the door. Filling the doorway was an enormous black man. Several inches taller than Kent and considerably broader, he must have weighed at least three hundred pounds.

Nonetheless, he looked strangely childish as he diffidently removed his cap and said, 'I came to see Cat.' Only then did Catherine look over to see who it was.

'My wife?'

'Brian!' Catherine spoke at the same time as Kent, jumping to her feet. A smile lit up her face as she crossed over to him, her hands extended. When she reached him, she threw her arms about him and received a bear-hug in return. When he released her, she stepped back and smiled at him. A former wrestler, he had blunt, homely features and skin the colour of burnished walnut. In the years since she had last seen him, his wiry black hair had thinned, but his most remarkable feature, aside from his size, was still a pair of gentle brown eyes set around a misshapen nose. His appearance, combined with his innate shyness, caused many people to dismiss him as an intellectual moron. However, in the years he had worked for Casey, Catherine had developed a healthy respect for his mental abilities. Brian was by no means the dumb ox he appeared to be, though he often adopted that role to his own advantage.

'Brian, it's so nice to see you again,' she said sincerely. Standing on tiptoe, she reached up and kissed his cheek. Her smile deepened as he grimaced in embarrassment and darted Kent a quick apologetic glance.

Turning to Kent, she saw his features were a mixture of apprehension and bewilderment. 'Kent, it's OK,' she said in an undertone, then louder, 'This is Brian Collins, he used to work for Casey. He's my friend. Brian, this is my husband, Kent Latimer.' She was secretly amused by the caution Kent couldn't hide as he extended his hand to the other man. Brian looked as though he could quite easily break every finger of her husband's hand when his great paw engulfed it.

A few minutes later the three of them were seated around the lounge. Catherine would have liked to have asked Peter to join them, but Kent had stayed her with a look. She supposed she couldn't blame him for being slightly suspicious of Brian. After Rick, he had every right to be wary of her past acquaintances.

Brian came abruptly to the point of his visit.

'What's this I hear on the Strip 'bout you goin' back to work for Rick, little girl?' he demanded.

'I am,' Catherine said quietly. She shot Kent a quick glance and saw that his mouth had firmed.

'He's a bad dude. I come to warn you to stay away from him.'

'I don't have any choice, Brian.'

'What's that moth . . . skunk,' he amended, 'been up to?'

Catherine spread her hands in a helpless gesture, then looked over to Kent. He was studying Brian thoughtfully, then suddenly he looked at her. 'I'm going to tell him, Cat.' He turned his attention back to the big black man. 'It's blackmail. He's threatened to expose how Cat's brother died. I don't know if you know this, but I'm interested in politics. If it came out, my career would be seriously damaged. At first, he just asked for money. Now, Cat doesn't think he'll accept it—that the only payment he'll agree to is having her go back to work for him.' Suddenly he met Catherine's eyes. 'It's not going to come to that. I have the money and if he won't take it, then it will just all have to come out. There'll be a scandal, but we'll weather it.'

Their eyes held. Kent's were dark, compelling blue and seemed to be saying all the things to her that he had never put into words. Gooseflesh formed along Catherine's arms, yet she felt as if somewhere inside her a fire had been kindled. Never before had he looked at her like this: as though she were the most important thing in his life; as though he loved her.

'Rick's bluffing. There ain't gonna be no scandal,' Brian's voice broke the moment of intimate communication and they pulled their attention back to him. But still it seemed to Catherine as if things weren't quite as bad as they had been before that exchanged look.

'I don't think he is, Brian,' she said regretfully.

'He is, because he's the one who'd fry if what happened ever came out. He and me were lyin' about Casey bein' on drugs.'

She stared at him, then shook her head in an unconscious gesture of denial. 'What do you mean, you were lying?'

'It wasn't true what we told you 'bout Casey. We didn't want you runnin' to the police and that was the only way we could think of to stop you.' Brian moved forward in his chair, resting his elbows on his knees, his eyes on her face. 'I'm sorry, Cat. I let Rick talk me into backin' him up. I don't think he knew you would quit, but I was pretty sure you would. If you hadn't of, I would have told you the truth then.'

'I don't think I understand,' Kent interposed.

Brian looked at him and asked, 'What do you know about Casey's death?'

Kent shrugged. 'That he died of an overdose. That Rick and Cat covered it up by making it look like a car accident.'

'I was there, too. I wish Cat hadn't of been. When we found him . . .' Brian rubbed his chin with one massive hand in a rueful gesture. 'We had to tell her sump'n, so we told her that Casey had been taking drugs for months. That way she wouldn't ask too many questions and would help us cover up how he really died. That was the lie we told, Cat.' Brian's tone compelled her to look at him. 'Casey was clean: he wasn't no junkie.'

'But . . .' she ran her hand through her hair

distractedly, 'I don't understand. He was dead. There was a needle there, all that other stuff. How . . .?'

'He was murdered, Cat.'

Long seconds ticked by in silence as Cat stared in blank disbelief at Brian, her face drained of all colour. Kent stood up and went to the liquor cabinet, returning a moment later with a glass of brandy. Pushing it into Catherine's hand, he enjoined her to drink it, then lifted his eyebrows in question to Brian. The other man nodded, so he returned to the cupboard and fixed them both a drink. Silently he handed one of the glasses to Brian, then settled on to the sofa next to Catherine, his arm going around her shoulders.

The brandy helped, warming her blood and dispelling the cold shock Brian's words had evoked. At last she was able to say, 'I want you to explain, Brian.' Her eyes were riveted on the other man's face.

Taking a sip of his drink, he nodded. 'It's a long story. I met Rick in New York 'bout fifteen years ago, though he was using a different name then. I worked for him. He was a loan shark and I was his collection agent, if you know what I mean. After a few months, I quit. I'm afraid I don't have the stomach for goin' around breakin' people's legs.' He frowned ruefully, lifting his glass to take another swallow of his drink. Presently he continued, 'I lost touch over the next few years until we met up again in Vegas. Only then he was Rick Moss, big-shot talent promoter and manager of the Devlins. When he asked me if I wanted the job as Casey's bodyguard, I was gonna turn it down. After New York, I spent a couple of years in prison, and I wanted to stay out of that place. I didn't want to get mixed up in sump'n crooked, but I met your brother and liked him and since Rick seemed to be stayin' clean, I took the job.'

He paused for a moment, swirling the ice cubes in his glass. 'By the time I found out what Rick was into, I had grown pretty attached to both you kids and didn't want to quit. I thought maybe I could keep you both out of trouble, protect you from Rick—but I guess I couldn't.' His blunt features hardened in anger and self-disgust.

'What was Moss doing?' asked Kent when Brian remained silent.

'On those trips Rick used to take, he brought back the occasional souvenir.' He looked up at them. 'He was a mule, smuggling coke and heroin. I found out what he was doin', but I knew enough to keep my mouth shut. Somehow, though, Casey found out,' he said flatly. 'For a kid who grew up on the streets, your brother was pretty damn stupid, Cat. He went to Rick and threatened to blow the whistle on him.'

'Are you saying that Rick——?'

'No, Cat. Rick ain't no murderer. Rick went to the dudes he was workin' for and told them Casey was causin' trouble. All he wanted was for them to scare him off. That was all, only . . .' Brian paused, draining his glass. 'Rick had been skimmin', holdin' back just a little of every delivery. He didn't think they knew, but they did. So they took out Casey. It shut him up and got back at Rick for cheatin' 'em.'

Brian set his empty glass on the table at his side, and shifted as though to rise. Kent said suddenly. 'What about you? Why did you keep quiet, help Rick cover up Casey's death?'

Brian sighed, running one large hand around the

back of his neck. 'You don't understand the sort of people Rick was dealin' with. My life or Cat's wouldn't have been worth two cents if we'd gone to the police with what really happened.' He paused, his face grim as he looked at Cat. 'Don't worry, though, little one. They didn't get away with it. You and Casey were the closest thing I ever had to a family. They were taken care of.'

Kent stared at the big black man in shock. 'You mean you . . .?'

Brian shrugged, then grinned. 'Heck, no . . . not that! After that stretch in the pen, I found out there are some things worse in life than death, and being locked up in that place is one of 'em. The guys that hurt my Casey are findin' that out. It wasn't that hard to find sump'n else on them, but I wanted Cat out of it first.'

He stood up abruptly. 'I'd better be goin'. Don't worry about Rick. I'll have a little talk with him. He won't be botherin' you again.' He stuck out his hand when Kent got to his feet and they shook hands firmly. 'I'm glad I met you. I've thought about Cat a lot in the past few years. It's good to know she's got somebody lookin' after her.' He turned to Cat, his big, homely face gentle, his eyes sad. 'I'm sorry, little girl, 'bout havin' to lie to you before, but it was the only thing I could think to do. You forgive me?'

Catherine smiled at him, her eyes misting. 'Of course I do. I understand,' she whispered. It wasn't easy to hug someone as big as Brian, but she wrapped her arms around him and squeezed. For a moment, he clasped her in his big, hamlike fists, then released her.

As he stepped back, Catherine detected a faint

sheen of moisture in his dark eyes. Looking sternly at Kent, he said in a rough voice, 'You look after her.' He turned and walked towards the door.

The silence that filled the room now that Brian had departed had a brooding quality to it. Catherine walked back to the sofa, picking up a cushion and plumping it idly. After a moment she clutched it to her stomach. Emotions tumbled around inside her, refusing to sort themselves out. Her joy in Casey's exoneration was blighted by guilt at her own misjudgment of him. He had not betrayed her, but she had betrayed him by believing he had done such a terrible thing.

Without her being aware of it, slow tears began to trickle down her cheeks. Five years! For five years of her life she had condemned him unjustly. If only she hadn't believed them!

An arm came around her shoulder and the pillow she had been clutching was pulled away. Kent gathered her to his chest, holding her against him with hard, protective arms. Catherine buried her face in his shoulder, her weeping intensifying as though a dam had burst inside her. Sobs raked through her and the arms holding her tightened. Kent murmured gently against her hair, his hand sliding beneath her hair to stroke the nape of her neck, attempting to soothe her. 'Come now, Cat, that's enough,' he said huskily.

She shook her head in a negative gesture. 'I shouldn't have believed them,' she said in a choked voice. 'I loved Casey, I should have known they were lying.'

'Cat.' He put his hands on her shoulders, easing her away from him. Seeing the tears still streaking down her cheeks, he gave her a little shake. Catherine bit her lip, forcing herself to control her tears. 'Listen to me, Cat,' Kent said sternly. 'You had to believe them. You heard what Brian said. Casey wouldn't have wanted you put in danger. He would have wanted you to be safe, even if it meant believing something like that. You've tortured yourself for five years because you thought he was an addict. I'm not going to let you torture yourself for the next five because he wasn't.'

She swallowed back a fresh wave of tears. 'I guess you're right.' She rested against him for several minutes and he stroked her hair comfortingly. Presently she said in a low voice, 'I'm sorry I put you through all this. I know how much your career means to you. I . . . I thought it would remain a secret, that— that if I never told anyone about Casey then—well, no one would know. And then it was too late. Will you forgive me?'

His hand stilled, then moved to her shoulder and carefully detached her from him. Holding her away from him, he peered into her face. 'Forgive you? If anyone needs to ask for forgiveness, it's me. My career . . .' Self-disgust flickered across his features. 'The pain I put you through in the name of my damned career! That night . . . when you cried in my arms, I felt something I'd never felt before. That's why I went to China. I was scared. And then, after making love to you for the first time, I was glad, Cat, glad you might be pregnant. It gave me an excuse to keep you with me for ever. And then when my father came here and told us about Rick . . . I had to face then what I'd been trying to do to you: to use you to advance my career, to throw you at my father to demonstrate my independence. Forcing you to marry me, go out with me. That night I had to face what it was costing you . . . and Cat . . .' he paused, swallowing with difficulty as his eyes darkened with contrition, 'when I left, went out for a time, it was because I was too ashamed to face you just then,' he admitted huskily. 'When I came back, all I wanted was to make it up to you, to protect you from that scum Rick, but . . .'

'I'd already agreed to work for him again,' Cat finished for him quietly.

He held her eyes in a steady gaze. 'I wouldn't let you go back to him knowing how you felt about him. No, even if Brian hadn't shown up when he did, that would never have happened.'

'But if Rick had released those pictures, told those lies.' A shudder passed through her. 'It would have been all over the papers. All your plans, your ambitions——'

'It wouldn't have mattered,' he cut her off. 'Don't you understand? I love you . . . it took me a long time to admit it, but I do. Cat, the night my father came here, I realised that by forcing you back into the limelight I was as responsible for making you as unhappy as Rick or your brother or anyone else. And that isn't love. I wanted to protect *you* from the scandal . . . not my career. When I told you I was worrying about a baby, it was only because I had to say something so that you would let me help you.'

'And I was trying to protect you! I love you so much and I didn't want you mixed up in that sordid mess. And then you and your father . . .'

'Stop worrying about my father,' Kent interrupted her severely. He slipped his finger under her chin and lifted it upwards. His mouth covered hers for a moment, then he said, 'That's the first time you've told me that . . . that you love me. Do you?'

Catherine smiled up at him, her eyes shining. Slowly she nodded.

A warm flame burned in the depths of his blue eyes as he returned her smile. 'In that case, we don't need to worry about anything. As long as we love each other.' For several minutes the room was silent as they expressed their feelings more convincingly than words ever could. When at last he released her, her lips were gently swollen and her cheeks faintly flushed. Slipping his arm around her, he led her towards the bedroom and opened the door.

They both stopped in astonishment at the sight that greeted them. Peter Castle was lying in the centre of the bed, his stockinged feet crossed and arms behind his head as he stared at the ceiling with a silly grin on his face. More startling, however, were the hundreds of loose bills piled over him and the bed.

Pointedly, Kent coughed. Instantly, Peter jack-knifed off the bed, scattering dollar bills in his wake, and flushing bright crimson. 'Oh, damm!' he exclaimed. 'I'd forgotten all about you two!' He gestured helplessly. Several more bills fluttered off the edge of the bed and he hastily made a grab at them as they fell to the floor.

'What in the world do you think you're doing?' Kent asked.

Peter straightened, his expression sheepish. 'Well, you see . . . you were in the other room for a long time and—well, I mean . . . I got bored and then—well, I've always had this fantasy . . .' He trailed off, his eyes moving wistfully to the mound of bills. 'I thought I'd have it all cleaned up again before you came in here.'

Catherine heard Kent make a choking sound in his throat and his expression remained stern as he looked at his friend. 'Do you realise that that is one hundred thousand dollars?' he demanded.

'I know, I guess that was what made it such a temptation! I never saw that kind of money all in pieces before.' Catherine saw Kent's lips twitch. 'Look,' Peter said quickly, 'I'm going to pick it all up. I'll count it and make sure I haven't lost any.'

Kent cleared his throat, then said, 'Don't bother. Cat and I will take care of it.' He paused. 'I have an errand for you. I want you to get over to Moss's before he skips town and pick up Cat's jewellery.' Peter's eyebrows shot up, but Kent only added, 'You shouldn't have any problem with him giving it to you. Just tell him you're a friend of Brian Collins.' He jerked his head towards the door. 'Now, how about getting out of here?'

Peter looked as though he would have liked to ask a few questions, but saw Kent's closed face and held them back. As soon as the door clicked shut behind him, Catherine released the giggle that had been threatening to choke her for the last few minutes. Kent's low chuckle joined in, then grew to a full-throated laugh as soon as the exterior door of the suite slammed.

Both their sides were aching when they finally got control of their mirth. Suddenly Kent eyed Catherine, then the money strewn over the bed. There was a wicked gleam in his eye. 'Have you ever had a fantasy, Cat?' he asked in a voice like silk. Without giving her a chance to answer, he lifted her off her feet and started towards the bed.

Harlequin Presents

Coming Next Month

1023 TOO SHORT A BLESSING Penny Jordan
After the tragic death of her fiancé, a young Englishwoman becomes
convinced that she'll never fall in love again—until she meets a very
determined man who has every intention of changing her mind...and
reaching her heart.

1024 MASQUERADE MARRIAGE Flora Kidd
On a Caribbean cruise, Carlotta discovers that the deckhand paying so much
attention to her is really a bodyguard hired by her wealthy father because
of kidnapping threats. The complication of their falling in love is not part of
the plan.

1025 CIRCLE OF FATE Charlotte Lamb
Things get complicated when Melanie, already doubtful about her
engagement to a prominent businessman, meets another man who infuriates
her, but also attracts her. Breaking off her engagement, however, doesn't
immediately bring about the desired results!

1026 A RACY AFFAIR Roberta Leigh
Emma Fielding, governess to a racing car driver's motherless child, is
persuaded to marry him so there'll be a guardian in case of his death. When
they fall in love with each other, they're too afraid at first to admit it.

1027 OUT OF THE SHADOWS Sandra Marton
When Lauren meets the man she knows is right for her, past bitterness
between their families threatens their love. Can they selfishly ignore the
hurtful consequences of their actions to achieve a happy future together?

1028 BRITTANY'S CASTLE Leigh Michaels
Successful banker Brittany Masters reluctantly agrees to a mock reconciliation
with her unfaithful husband until he obtains a government appointment. In
return he'll give her a divorce. The situation is awkward, but happily nothing
turns out as they expect.

1029 NO STRINGS ATTACHED Annabel Murray
When lively, actively social, travel agent Vita, believing in love and commitment,
meets attractive but footloose Dominic, looking for a temporary affair, conflict
is inevitable. So, too, is love—but in between is a time of turmoil.

1030 TOUCH AND GO Elizabeth Oldfield
That it turns out to be a hoax, doesn't make her stepfather's kidnapping any
less harrowing for Karis, visiting him in Bangkok. Especially when the only one
she can turn to is the man she'd loved and broken off with six months before.

Available in November wherever paperback books are sold, or through
Harlequin Reader Service:

In the U.S.
901 Fuhrmann Blvd.
P.O. Box 1397
Buffalo, N.Y. 14240-1397

In Canada
P.O. Box 603
Fort Erie, Ontario
L2A 5X3

What the press says about Harlequin romance fiction...

"When it comes to romantic novels...
Harlequin is the indisputable king."
  —*New York Times*

"...always with an upbeat, happy ending."
  —*San Francisco Chronicle*

"Women have come to trust these
stories about contemporary people,
set in exciting foreign places."
  —*Best Sellers*, New York

"The most popular reading matter of
American women today."
  —*Detroit News*

"...a work of art."
  —*Globe & Mail*, Toronto

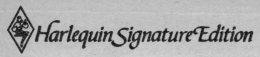

Harlequin Signature Edition

Penny Jordan

Stronger Than Yearning

He was the man of her dreams!

The same dark hair, the same mocking eyes; it was as if the Regency rake of the portrait, the seducer of Jenna's dream, had come to life. Jenna, believing the last of the Deverils dead, was determined to buy the great old Yorkshire Hall—to claim it for her daughter, Lucy, and put to rest some of the painful memories of Lucy's birth. She had no way of knowing that a direct descendant of the black sheep Deveril even existed—or that James Allingham and his own powerful yearnings would disrupt her plan entirely.

Penny Jordan's first Harlequin Signature Edition *Love's Choices* was an outstanding success. Penny Jordan has written more than 40 best-selling titles—more than 4 million copies sold.

Now, be sure to buy her latest bestseller, *Stronger Than Yearning*. Available wherever paperbacks are sold—in October.

An enticing
new historical romance!

Spring Will Come

SHERRY DeBORDE

It was 1852, and the steamy South was in its last hours of
gentility. Camille Braxton Beaufort went searching for the
one man she knew she could trust, and under his protec-
tion had her first lesson in love....